THE
JEWELS of CYTTORAK

THE
JEWELS of CYTTORAK

DEAN WESLEY SMITH

ILLUSTRATIONS BY
CHUCK WOJTKIEWICZ

BYRON PREISS MULTIMEDIA COMPANY, INC.
NEW YORK

BOULEVARD BOOKS, NEW YORK

X-MEN: THE JEWELS OF CYTTORAK

A Boulevard Book
A Byron Preiss Multimedia Company, Inc. Book

Special thanks to Ginjer Buchanan, Steve Roman, Michelle LaMarca, Howard Zimmerman, Emily Epstein, Ursula Ward, Mike Thomas, and Steve Behling.

PRINTING HISTORY
Boulevard paperback edition/December 1997

All rights reserved.
Copyright © 1997 Marvel Characters, Inc.
Edited by Keith R. A. DeCandido.
Cover design by Claude Goodwin.
Cover art by Vince Evans.
Interior design by Michael Mendelsohn.
This book may not be reproduced in whole or in part,
by mimeograph or any other means, without permission.
For information address: Byron Preiss Multimedia Company, Inc.,
24 West 25th Street, New York, New York 10010.

The Putnam Berkley World Wide Web site address is
http://www.berkley.com

Check out the Byron Preiss Multimedia Co., Inc. site on the World
Wide Web: http://www.byronpreiss.com

Make sure to check out *PB Plug*, the science fiction/fantasy newsletter,
at http://www.pbplug.com

ISBN: 1-57297-329-3

BOULEVARD
Boulevard Books are published by The Berkley Publishing Group,
a member of Penguin Putnam Inc.,
200 Madison Avenue, New York, New York 10016.
BOULEVARD and its logo
are trademarks belonging to Berkley Publishing Corporation.

PRINTED IN THE UNITED STATES OF AMERICA

10 9 8 7 6 5 4 3 2 1

For

Steve and Chris,
Thanks for all the good friendship

PROLOGUE

The intense heat and mist-thick humidity smothered the jungle like a blanket tucked in tight on all four corners of a bed. All noises were muffled and everything was wet to the touch. Just simple breathing seemed harder than normal. Even the light of the sun fought to get through the thick air to warm the damp ground.

Two brown-robed monks were the only life moving this hot afternoon, as they walked with their faces turned downward at the moist soil of the jungle floor. The thin, rough fabric of their robes clung to them, showing wet outlines of legs and arms. Sweat coated both their faces, dripping from their chins. Their eyes were blank, their pace measured, controlled through the thick heat.

The path curved ahead of them like a snake winding its way around trees and brush. The two had walked this path every day for the past nine years, but always much earlier in the morning, just after dawn, when the mist and the air still had a slight touch of coolness to it.

And before today they had always walked it with many others of their order. Never had they gone alone before. The others would be shocked if they knew.

The two monks would be shocked if they understood their own actions.

But they did not. They simply moved like zombies, one step at a time through the humidity, drawn to a task they were unaware of doing.

The path turned upward and moved out of the jungle, twisting back and forth past rocks, climbing toward a stone temple half-built, half-carved from the face of the rock bluff. The temple dominated the valley below on clear days, seeming to rule over the world of real life in the jungle.

On closer inspection, the temple looked ancient and was in desperate need of repair, but there was no one to repair it. The great structure had been built by an unknown people ages before the two monks were born. No records or stories of the temple's builders had passed down through the centuries.

Only a name: Cyttorak.

It was a sacred place, the temple of Cyttorak.

A place of great power.

A place that allowed mere men to feel closer to their god. Only the monks dared go inside, and only during the early morning hours. After that, not even the monks entered the sacred place.

Until today.

Now, the two monks blindly followed the path, not looking forward or upward at the temple of Cyttorak, only down at their feet, as if ashamed of what they were about to attempt. And they would have been ashamed, if they had been aware.

But the power of Cyttorak had reached them. And now drew them to a task.

They were to be the vessels that would carry the power of Cyttorak into the world.

A hundred paces behind the two monks another monk followed, staying to the edge of the trail, ready to duck behind a brush or tree at any moment. Unlike the two young monks being drawn to the temple, he was old, his beard gray. For his entire life, he and the other elders of the monastery had waited for this day. And worried about it happening.

For centuries, the elder monks had guarded the temple, passing down the guard duty generation after generation.

Now, during his time of watch, it was happening. Cyttorak was again calling to younger members of the order, as had been foretold. It was his duty to stop the calling by any means possible.

Other elders would be following to help, but they might not arrive in time. Fear gripped him, but he forced it aside and moved on after the two young monks. He had spent his life preparing for this moment. He would not fail now.

The temple held the heat of the day outside, stopping it at the door like an unwanted guest. The air inside was deathly still between the stone walls. It smelled of mold and ancient death. The high stone ceilings and massive construction gave any visitor the sense of immense power around them, looming like a dark figure in the night. It was a humbling feeling to the few who had seen the insides of the sacred place.

The two young monks entered through the main arch and moved slowly down the central corridor of the temple, not glancing around. Sweat dripped down their backs and arms, but they felt no discomfort. Their eyes remained blank, not seeing their true location, not seeing anything.

During the usual morning worships, they always turned right at the end of the corridor and into the large hall with its open windows and stone pillars.

This time they turned left at that spot and stopped at the statue of a deformed creature sitting on a throne. The creature's head was rounded and without neck. Snakelike bands wrapped around under its arms and extended into the air behind its head. Its chest was massive, its arms huge and ending in fists.

The name of the creature was said to be lost in time and the passing of the temple's builders. None of the younger monks could have imagined that the monster sitting in the huge throne-like chair was Cyttorak. If they had, they would have never entered the temple again.

But the elders knew. And they knew that their duty, their life's work, was to keep Cyttorak inside that stone temple.

The two younger monks had accidentally discovered the temple's secret late one morning. They had heard a noise near the statue as the order was leaving for the morning. They had stopped and investigated, thinking a village child had found his or her way inside the sacred place.

They had accidentally, or so it seemed at the time, pushed on both arms of the statue's chair at the same moment. The stone wall and statue of the creature had moved inward and back, opening a walkway that led downward.

The two young monks had entered and moved down

the stone stairs as the wall slid closed behind them. At the bottom of exactly one hundred stairs, they found a bitterly cold room and a sight that had scared them. They had quickly returned to the light of day and the heat of the jungle, but just the visit to the room had allowed Cyttorak to cross over between the two worlds and gain a small measure of control of their young minds.

Over the next two weeks, Cyttorak solidified that control every morning when they came for their morning service, until finally the two monks would do as he bid.

They would return to the room and set him free.

As the two young monks disappeared into the mouth of the tunnel, the older monk stopped and stared at the opening, his stomach turning in fear. He knew what they would find below. He had never seen it. None of the monks now living had seen that room except the two young ones. Now he was about to go down into a place he had prayed to never enter: the sacred throne room of Cyttorak.

He forced himself to take a deep breath to calm his shaking hands. He stepped to a hidden alcove and retrieved a large wooden staff. The elders had all trained for years in the art of fighting with the staffs, and there were many hidden along the path to this temple in case they were needed. He had always hoped to never have to touch one outside of the training room, but now that the solid wooden weapon was in his hands, he felt better.

Quickly, he moved in past the statue and down the stairs after the two younger monks, hoping that he would be in time to stop them.

• • •

At the bottom of the stairs, light from the outside sliced through the huge dark room from four round holes bored at angles through the rock above. Two of the shafts of light focused on the eyes of a gigantic statue of the same deformed creature that guarded the tunnel entrance above. It was as if the creature, through the shafts of light, always looked out into the world.

The elder monks believed he did.

And since finding the room the first time, the two younger monks had never lost the feeling of being watched. Now, directed by some unseen hand, they had returned to a place they had hoped to never have to see again.

The other two spots of light focused on the monster's hands, and the two huge stones he held in his palms. In his right a huge emerald, in his left an equally large ruby. Both stones were larger than a man's closed fist and under the light both seemed to have a life and energy all their own.

In reality, they were gateways to the mystic power bands of Cyttorak. The two stones, when touched by the same person, would allow Cyttorak to come through the barrier between his world and the human one. And with his power there would be nothing humanity could do to stop him from ruling the world. Nothing.

But the young monks did not know this. Their eyes were blank, their bodies controlled by Cyttorak.

They stopped, facing the huge statue of Cyttorak, as if worshipping their new god. Then the young monk on the right stepped forward, both hands outstretched, reaching for the gems held out for him by the huge creature.

"No!" the elder monk shouted from the doorway.

The shout seemed to have no effect on the spell over the two young monks.

With a quick step forward and a swing of the staff, the elder monk smashed the closest young monk in the head with the staff. The young man went down like a stone.

Then, with a quick spin, the older monk knocked away one arm of one younger monk, obviously breaking it with the force of his blow.

But the younger monk continued to reach for the emerald, as if he didn't feel the pain from his smashed arm.

"I said no!" the older monk shouted.

But the younger monk was within an inch of touching the huge gem.

With a quick swipe with the staff, the older monk tried to knock the hand away from the stone. But in his excitement and rush, he missed.

And hit the emerald.

The room exploded in green light.

The elder monk stepped back.

It was as if the room had suddenly filled with the anger of centuries. Anger, now fueled with the frustration of failure, released in a huge explosion by an errant hit with a staff.

The energy increased quickly, burning the skin off the three monks before they could even feel the pain.

The intense blast of the energy released from the emerald quickly boiled away their blood and then turned their bones to a fine dust that filled the swirling air of the room like the mist in the hot, thick air outside.

The emerald grew brighter and brighter.

Then suddenly it shattered into three pieces in a huge explosion that sent huge stones flying. The ground shook and rocks filled the stairway to the temple above.

One large piece of the emerald was quickly buried in the stone wall of the hidden room.

The other two pieces, fueled by the otherdimensional power of Cyttorak, were sent spinning through space and time into the future.

After a moment, the dust from the monks' bones settled and only one light shaft still shown down on the creature, now holding only a bright ruby, as if offering it to the first person who would come along and take it.

It would be centuries, long after the temple had crumpled into a pile of stones and Cyttorak was only a long-ago memory, before Cain Marko came along and did just that.

CHAPTER 1

In the dead-of-night hours, the French Quarter in New Orleans was a place of danger and excitement. The party and business life of the day and evening still echoed through the empty spaces of Jackson Square. The laughter and the jazz were now only ghosts drifting among the tall old trees and vine-covered buildings. The heat and the humidity lingered over the rough pavement of the streets. Not even the darkness could push it back to a cooler time.

The black shadows just outside the streetlights gave the park a feeling of secrets lost and danger to come. Tourists who walked near Jackson Park in the late hours walked quickly, sensing the danger, their hearts beating hard from the brush against imagined death. But it was that very closeness to the unknown, wrapped in the history of the old town, that brought them back the following year. Brought them back to the parties, back to the great Cajun cooking, back to the unknown danger just inside the nearest shadow or the closest hidden courtyard.

Remy LeBeau, aka Gambit, knew every shadow, every alley, every courtyard tucked behind iron gates. For years he had been part of those shadows, a part of the very real danger the tourists had feared. New Orleans was his home, the streets of the French Quarter his back yard.

And now, again, he had returned home, to the town he loved more than anything else in the world. But his return was not a joyous one. Something was wrong with his home city.

Very wrong.

He just didn't know what.

A disturbing call from an unknown "friend" had brought him from the Xavier Institute in New York—Gambit's new home among the super-team known as the X-Men—back to the Big Easy.

The "friend" had said only that the power was no longer in the Guilds in New Orleans. That now a man named Toole controlled things. And Toole did not understand the old ways.

The caller had hung up with no explanation as to how he had found Remy, or why he had even called. Remy knew he still had friends in the Guilds even though he was long ago outcast. More than likely it was one of them.

So he had gone home, and now the night air of New Orleans again wrapped him in its friendly thickness, the heat holding him like a mother would hold a child as he searched for clues.

He moved past Jackson Square and ducked into a shadowed alcove where he could watch the back entrance to a private club called the Bijou. The place had been there since before Remy was born. The wooden tables were scarred with the burns of too many cigarette butts, the wooden floor warped from years of spilled drinks. Remy knew the air would be filled with a gray smoke that even during the early morning hours never seemed to clear. In the back room, a poker game would be going on continuously. In his memory, that back room had never been without a game.

Twenty minutes later, Remy's wait ended as a trench-coated figure appeared from the dark passage and stepped onto the sidewalk. He glanced both directions down the dark street and then turned to the right, away from the park, his hands deep in the pockets of his coat.

Remy knew the guy only as "York." A tall, heavy-set man with blond hair, York had moved down from Chicago when he was twenty and had managed to survive. He was now a small-time player who ran a bookmaking operation across the river. Sanctioned by the Guilds and ignored by the cops, York kept his nose clean, staying only with his book. His only vice was that he liked to gamble away his profits and most likely had been doing just that tonight, in the famous back room of the Bijou.

Remy stepped from the shadow and quietly moved across the street behind the tall man, unheard and unseen. He had his own coat buttoned and his hand on two of his playing cards in his pocket, just in case York did something really stupid. Gambit had the power to charge any article with extreme kinetic energy that was released in a very destructive force on impact. A simple playing card, when charged and flicked, carried more destructive force than a bullet fired from a handgun.

"Y'ever hear de streets are dangerous, *mon ami*?" Remy asked as he neared the large man.

York spun, his right hand clearly holding a gun in the pocket of his trench coat.

"Kinda jumpy dere, York," Remy said, smiling at the big man.

"LeBeau?" York asked, lowering his gun hand slightly, but not yet letting it go.

And Remy didn't let go of the cards just yet, either.

"Y'expectin' someone else?"

York shook his head, then took a deep breath. "You just startled me. What are you doing back here? Bella?"

The mention of his wife's name jolted Remy. Bella Donna had recovered after being killed because he'd given her the sacred elixir of life. But when she awoke she had lost all memory of him. Now she had taken over as the head of the Assassins Guild. He was a thief, she an assassin. The two Guilds were sworn enemies from generations back. No, he was not here for Bella, and until now he had managed to keep thoughts of her pushed back.

"*Non*," Remy said clearly and firmly. "Just a little of de information."

York had now dropped his hand completely, but Remy knew he still held his gun. But Remy also knew that York was too smart to move against him.

"I'll tell you what I can," York said, glancing around at the dark street to see if anyone was watching.

Remy knew that someone was watching, but he said nothing to the big man.

"Toole?" Remy said.

Even in the shadows and faint light of the street, Remy could see York's face go pale. He quickly glanced again in both directions down the street, then stepped a half step closer to Remy.

"The guy's a monster," York said, his voice a harsh whisper. "Came into town about a year ago when they started one of the river gambling boats. He controls his people like they were puppets and ignores the old ways completely."

"And nobody yanked his leash?" Remy couldn't believe that the Guilds or the police hadn't stopped the growth of a new crime boss. The power here had been balanced and working for such a long time, someone like Toole running loose could easily cause a bloodbath.

York shook his head. "I heard they tried a couple of times, but the guy has power. Almost unnatural power. He's like a cancer eating at things, LeBeau."

Remy nodded. "Where I find dis fellow?"

York shook his head. "That's another thing about him. People don't find him, he finds them. Like a ghost."

Remy only snorted. "Where, *mon ami*?"

York looked a little panicked for a moment, then recovered. "Best I heard was that he had a warehouse down the river a ways, armed like a fortress. No one gets in."

Remy laughed. He was a thief. And one of the best, if not the best there had ever been. His training was to get in places where no one else did, and do it without being seen.

York again glanced around as if afraid someone might be watching, then turned to Remy. "Look, it's been good seeing you, but I got to go."

Remy only nodded and York looked relieved.

"Good luck," York said and turned in the direction he'd been heading.

Remy stepped silently back into the shadows of a doorway and a moment later when York glanced around it was clear from his surprise that he couldn't see Remy. LeBeau knew that, to York, he had simply disappeared off the street, an old thief's trick.

But a harder trick was going to be disappearing from the person who had watched their conversation. The person standing in the shadows half a block up the street.

Remy had known he was there the entire time. Now to find out who he was.

The rotting-flesh stench of the dying man seemed to fill every corner of the sterile, white room. The smell was thick, choking, and almost sweet. It covered the hospital bed, the nightstand, and the four high-tech monitoring machines against the wall like a thick film in a drunk's mouth after a long night's binge. During the day, the smell was almost bearable, with the air conditioners going and the windows open, but now, late at night, the room was closed up and the smell seemed to be even thicker than normal.

A rail-thin nurse with pale skin sat in a chair in front of the bank of machines and Gary Service, the younger son of the dying man, sat in a chair beside the bed.

Robert Service, the older son, stood in the door, the smell keeping him out of the room like a wall. Somehow he hoped that a slight breeze of fresh air would cover him from the hall. He couldn't imagine how his brother stood the smell that close to the old man for as long as he did. It seemed the kid was always at the old man's side, helping the nurses, talking with the doctors.

Robert, on the other hand, stayed in his office most of the time, on the far side of the huge Service mansion. He ignored the fact that his father was being eaten slowly by a nasty form of skin cancer. Someone had to watch after the family businesses, and with the old man dying, and Gary worthless when it came to such things, he was the one.

And it suited him.

Business in America was a ruthless place, where only the strong survived. And Robert considered himself ruthless. He planned on being one of the strong the day the old man passed into the next life. If Robert had his way, the Service millions would soon become the Service billions.

The old man moaned and Gary looked up. Robert had to admit that the kid looked tired. His green eyes were circled with dark rings and his hair was uncombed. He had some sort of orange food on his shirt from helping dear old dad eat. The kid had a heart and he cared about the old man for some reason. And that was Gary's biggest problem. He had a heart. He would never make a good businessman.

"He's coming around again," Gary said, standing up so that he stood beside the old man, almost hovering. Beside the bed a faint *beep-beep-beep* signaled a slight increase in the old man's heart rate. For some reason the old man had asked them both to be here, at this late hour of the night. Robert had no idea why, but that was true of many things his father did.

"Good," Robert said. He managed to choke back his disgust at the rotting smell of human flesh and moved a step into the room and closer to the bed. The old man had given him instructions to bring a large sealed package from the old man's personal safe. It now rested on the stand near the bed.

For two years, Robert had wondered what was in the heavy package, and had been looking forward to opening it the day his father died. Now it seemed he was going to get the chance to see the contents just a little sooner than expected.

The old man opened his eyes and slowly let them focus on the ceiling. There was still a hardness to those gray eyes. In his nightmares, Robert would see those eyes glaring at him as the old man took his belt and hit him over and over. Twice a week for years, Robert had survived the old man's beatings, while Gary never seemed to be touched by the belt. Never hit by the old man. It would be a joyous day, as far as Robert was concerned, when his father never opened those vicious, gray eyes again.

"Good," the old man said, his voice hoarse. "You're both here. Send the nurse away."

With a wave of his hand, Robert chased the woman in white out of the room and closed the door behind her, trapping himself with the rotting smell, his dying father, and his weak brother.

"You brought the package?" his father asked, his voice gaining strength at the same time as the beeping from the machine increased in speed.

"On the nightstand beside you," Robert said.

"Open it, please, Gary," the old man said, his voice now firm and in control.

Robert watched as Gary pulled open the tape and the brown paper wrapping from the package. Inside was an ornate wooden box, about the size of a woman's travel jewelry case. A wax seal covered the edge of the box, molded over a thin clasp. From what Robert could tell, the box hadn't been opened in years.

"The jewel of the temple of Cyttorak," the old man

said, staring at the still unopened box. "It must never be touched."

"What?" Robert asked, stepping closer to the bed and the box, even though the smell pushed at him.

"Father," Gary said, putting a hand gently on the decaying skin of the old man's arm. "I think you should start from the beginning."

The old man nodded. "Open the box first. And be careful to not touch the jewel."

Gary nodded and used his fingernail to slice open the wax seal covering a small brass latch. Then he slowly raised the lid.

Robert gasped.

Gary said, "Oh, my."

Inside the box, on a soft bed of white silk, was the largest emerald Robert had ever seen. At least half the size of his fist. It seemed to fill the area around the box with a green glow, as if it had an energy all its own.

Robert stepped over closer to his brother and stared at the emerald. The thing had to be worth millions, at least. He wanted more than anything to reach down and pick up the wonderful-looking stone.

"Be very careful," the old man said. "You must never touch the emerald. Ever."

Robert glanced at the old man who kept repeating the same craziness. *The cancer must finally be getting to his brain*, he thought. Robert moved back away from the choking smell of the dying man. "I think it's time for that story, now."

The old man nodded.

"It happened back when I was stationed in Korea

with the Army Corps of Engineers. My unit was working on building a bunker in what looked to be the remains of an old temple built into a rock cliff. One hot morning, out of the blue, an old monk approached us and told us a story of the former god of the temple, a monstrous being named Cyttorak.''

"Doesn't sound like a Korean name to me," Robert said.

"It's not," the old man said. "The monk told us the god was before time, and not from our world. He said the temple was not a place for man."

"And you believed him?"

"Of course not," the old man said, snorting, then coughing at the effort. After a moment he went on. "When it became clear we would not leave, the old monk warned us that if we should find any gems, to never touch them, for fear of setting Cyttorak free on the earth again."

"Setting him free, huh?" Robert laughed.

His father ignored the interruption and continued. "Then the monk left. We got a good laugh from the story and went back to work."

Robert nodded. From his memory of his hard-nosed father, that sounded right. More likely they ran the old monk off into the trees at gunpoint, but there was no reason to suggest that now.

"Three days later, while exploring a caved-in area under the temple, we found an old statue. It was a huge chunk of carved rock that showed an ugly beast of a creature sitting on a throne. His hands were extended outward, as if at one time he'd been holding something in each."

"Let me guess," Robert said. "Cyttorak."

"Most likely," the old man said, ignoring the sarcasm in his son's voice. "It sure spooked about half my crew. Over the years that we were in that godforsaken country, my crew and I had seen a lot of strange things. That statue in that old temple was one of the strangest."

"So, Father," Gary said, "how'd you find the emerald?"

"Not exactly sure," he said, shaking his head from side to side. "All I remember is it being late at night and I found myself being drawn up to our construction area. The two guards I had posted on the place startled me awake, as if I'd been sleepwalking or something."

"Not a good thing to be doing in Korea," Robert said. "At least from what I have heard about the place."

The father choked out a half laugh. "You have that right."

"Go on," Gary said, again touching the rotting flesh of the old man.

The old man looked for a long moment at the glowing emerald in its case on the medical stand, then went on with his story. "I decided that there must have been something drawing me there that night, so I went ahead and did a quick inspection of our bunker, just to see if anything was wrong. After the inspection, I found myself wandering back into the old temple and down near the statue. In the darkness, I spotted the green glow coming from one wall right across from the statue. When I dug at the glow with a shovel, the emerald dropped out."

"And you didn't touch it?" Gary asked.

"I almost did," the old man said. "I wanted to."

"Then you remembered the monk's words, right?"

Robert said, managing not to laugh at the story.

"Actually, that's right," the old man said, glaring with those cold gray eyes at Robert.

Robert only returned the stare and after a moment his father looked away, glancing at the emerald before he continued.

"I picked up the emerald with a shovel, wrapped it in some cloth, and stuck it in a backpack. I never told a person about it until today."

"All because of the words of a monk almost thirty years ago?" Robert asked.

The old man only nodded, his eyes going slightly vacant, as if telling the story had taken some of the last of his strength.

"And you didn't use the gem as collateral to help build our business? You just kept it hidden?" Robert couldn't believe that his father wouldn't have used such a valuable gem to his best advantage, especially since he came back from Korea totally broke and built a million-dollar fortune since.

"That's right," the old man said. "No one has seen it until tonight. Not even your mother, God rest her soul."

"Well," Robert said, "I don't intend to let a stupid legend stop me from having this stone checked out."

With two quick steps through the thick smell of cancer-rotting flesh, he moved to where Gary had placed the box on the medicine table near the bed.

"No!" the old man said.

Gary moved to stop him, but far too late.

He reached into the box and picked up the green emerald of Cyttorak.

His first thought was that the old man must have wired the gem with an electrical current. His hand froze to the surface of the stone like a kid's tongue to an ice-covered flagpole.

The energy charged his arm, filling his chest and head with a feeling of strength, like nothing he had never felt before.

Then the energy surged, as if the first jolt had only been a faint test.

He screamed and closed his eyes as the energy pushed and shoved its way into his body, filling him like a balloon, pushing out at his skin as if trying to make him explode.

And then, as if suddenly opening his eyes on a new day, he understood what was happening. He was becoming stronger, bigger, more powerful than ever before.

Yet there was something missing. As his strength and energy increased, he could sense that it was only a part of the full power he might have. He knew that the stone he'd touched was only part of what had once been a larger stone. And that now that he had touched the stone, he needed the other parts, more than he needed anything else. He would never be complete until he had them all together.

With a sudden snap the surging energy from the emerald let him go.

He slowly opened his eyes.

His father and brother both cowered together, staring up at him, their eyes wide, their mouths open.

The room around him seemed strange now to him, as if he were looking at it from another perspective. With a quick glance around, then down at his own tattered clothes, he realized what had happened.

He had physically gotten bigger.

Much bigger.

He squeezed his hands and stretched his arms.

Much stronger, too.

Where before he could have never reached the seven-foot ceiling of the room, now he touched it without a problem.

He glared down at his father and enjoyed the look of fear in those awful gray eyes. It was a look he'd never seen in them before and it pleased him.

"Are—are you all right?" Gary asked, his voice shaking with fear.

"Better than ever," he said. His voice was so loud it shook the machines monitoring his father.

He held up the emerald and studied it. Now it didn't seem to glow as it had moments before. Its energy had transferred to him. He knew that, as he knew that this was only a fragment of a much more powerful stone.

As he knew he would never rest until he had the remaining parts of the emerald.

He laughed and his laugh seemed to fill the room and shake the curtains pulled over the window. Now he would be stronger and more powerful than he had ever hoped. And that extra power fit right in with his plans to be the richest and most powerful man alive.

"I warned you—" his father said.

"And like always, Father," Robert said, bellowing down at the old man, "you were wrong. If you'd have touched your precious emerald, you wouldn't be lying there rotting away like a dead fish in the hot sun. But now there is nothing you can do, is there? I'm no longer a child to be beaten at your whim. Now, I'm the strong one. How does it feel, *Father*?''

The old man's face was filled with intense fear as he stared up from his bed.

The beeping on the heart monitor intensified and suddenly shrill alarms sounded.

''Nurse!'' Gary shouted as the old man clutched his chest and snapped his eyes closed in response to the pain.

Robert only laughed, then turned and headed for the door, the emerald in his hand. He had work to do, an empire to build. And two more parts of the emerald to find to complete his power.

At the door he had to duck to pass through. And that made him laugh all the way to his office.

CHAPTER 2

There were longer and longer stretches of time in which Cain Marko's greatest desire was to just be left alone.

As a kid growing up with a sadistic father, Cain was often left alone. And back then he didn't want it that way. Then, all he wanted was a kind word from his father, a show of any sort of affection, any kind of positive attention. But what he got were cold looks, indifference, and physical abuse. So much coldness in fact that he grew up hating his family. He hated his father for his coldness, his stepmother for her weakness, and his stepbrother Charles for the favoritism his father showed because the little kid was smart.

But now, years later, as the Juggernaut, he more often than not just wanted to be left alone with his own thoughts and the peace of each day. It hadn't been that way when he had first become the Juggernaut. Then all he had wanted to do was smash things. Anything that got in his way. Or even thought of getting in his way.

That had been years ago. Now, peace and quiet was sufficient.

But today, as with many other times over the years, peace and quiet wasn't to be.

Around him the warm day and thick, humid air wrapped the Ohio countryside in a sense of serenity. He had found an old, abandoned farmhouse sitting in some ragged trees on a slight rise. From the looks of the well-tended fields around it, some larger farm had bought this one and just left the family house to crumble with time. Now the paint was long since scoured from the wood, leaving it gray and cracked. The roof leaked and rats had built nests in the walls. Marko felt almost sorry for the place. At some time in the past the old place looked to have held a family. Maybe even a happy family. Marko could only hope.

Now, for Cain Marko, the Juggernaut, the old farmhouse was perfect. He had spent the last two days just hanging out around the old building, enjoying the quiet. In the mornings he wandered the fields and the nearby dirt roads, in the afternoon he sat on what remained of the back porch, just leaning against the building and staring out over the land. Two days now and it had been the longest stretch of peacefulness that he could remember. And if he got his way, he'd just stay right here for the summer.

He had just returned to the porch after a walk and was just sitting his huge frame gently down on the old, faded wood, when the pain hit.

Pain in his chest, almost like he would have imagined a heart attack might feel like.

But he was the Juggernaut. He didn't feel pain.

And he would never have a heart attack, not as long as the Crimson Ruby of Cyttorak was attached to his chest.

He had felt impacts in fights in the past, but never pain, not since the day he'd picked up the ruby in that old temple. It had transformed him into the Juggernaut, an unstoppable force. And with his armor, including his helmet, nothing could hurt him.

Now suddenly, something was hurting him.

He grabbed his chest and roared, shaking the old building around him.

But the pain didn't diminish.

Or increase.

He pounded on his chest as if he were playing King Kong climbing the Empire State Building, hoping to knock the pain out and away.

That didn't change it.

It was just a solid aching pain around the ruby on his chest. And it was starting to make him mad.

Really mad.

He smashed a fist through the wood floor of the porch, then stopped.

He forced himself to take a deep breath.

Come on, pal, he said to himself. *Get a grip. Breaking up this old place ain't gonna help.*

Another big, deep breath and he could sense something. A direction? Was the pain coming from the outside?

"Weird," he said aloud.

He stood and moved out into the open grassy area that had once been the farmhouse's front yard. There he stopped, facing south, and took a third deep breath to calm his anger just a touch.

Nothing. The pain continued, just like he remembered feeling from a bad toothache he'd had when he was a kid. His father had ignored his requests to go to a dentist for three days. Three days of intense pain that Cain remembered very clearly.

Now he was feeling that same kind of pain again.

And he didn't like it today anymore than he did then.

When the Juggernaut didn't like something, he pounded on it until there was nothing left to pound on. Somehow, he'd find what was causing this pain and pound it like he'd never pounded anything before.

He took another deep breath and turned to face west.

He wasn't sure, but it felt as if the pain might have increased slightly. It was as if the ruby was trying to tell him something, but he couldn't understand. He had never really gained any increased intelligence from the ruby, only massive strength.

He quickly turned to the north and the pain went back to its original level. And now he could sense a little more. Something was interfering with the power into the ruby. Something was cutting at the bands of Cyttorak where his power came from. He knew that, but he didn't know how he knew that.

For the first time in a very long time, he was worried. If the power of the ruby was cut, he'd just be a regular human being again. Someone who could be hurt and killed. He'd been the Juggernaut for so long he could no longer imagine just being a regular human. There was no way he was going to let that happen without a fight, that was for sure.

He faced east and the pain went down slightly. Inside his head he could sense that was the right direction, as if something through the stone was telling him so.

So east it was.

Without a look back at the abandoned farmhouse, he started off across the field, paying no attention to what was in his way ahead.

THE JEWELS OF CYTTORAK

Nothing was going to stop him until he found out who or what was causing him this pain.

And then he would stop it. Hard.

Gary Service took a long, deep breath and stepped back away from his father's death bed. The nurse had managed to calm the old man enough to stop the heart attack from being serious and give him some medication. Now he slept, his breath wheezing in and out, once in a while catching, making Gary wonder if that was the last breath for old man Service, or not.

Gary felt numb inside.

He forced himself to move out into the hall and down toward the darkened kitchen. What had happened to Robert was not something he could have even imagined. As always, Robert had been angry, defying their father at every turn. And Gary would have expected that if the old man said, "Don't touch," then Robert would touch.

Gary laughed aloud and the sound echoed off the polished wooden floor and high ceilings of the hallway. Maybe the old man had *wanted* Robert to touch the gem after all. Maybe the old man figured it would serve Robert right, but it was clear the result was not what the old man had expected. Not at all.

It was not a result anyone in the world would have expected, or believed.

But it had happened. Robert had touched the emerald and been suddenly filled with a bright green energy of some sort that became so bright that it hurt Gary's eyes to watch. Then Robert had simply grown in an impossible manner, from a normal five-foot-ten, to six-and-a-half feet tall. And muscled, as if he had been lifting weights for ten years. It was like something that happened only in a special effect on television, or to some New York super hero, not in the real world. People don't just grow in front of your eyes.

But Robert had.

Gary slowly moved into the huge kitchen, shaking his head at the insanity of what he had seen. He retrieved a tall glass and filled it with milk, then grabbed some freshly baked chocolate-chip cookies. Robert always snorted at Gary's childhood habit of milk and cookies, but Gary loved it, and if it helped Robert continue to believe that Gary was weak and young and stupid, so much the better.

Robert would soon find out different. He was in for a big surprise when the old man died and Robert discovered that Gary owned fifty-one percent of the Service businesses. And he would be even more surprised when Gary stepped in and ran the business with the intent of giving all the profits and eventually all the business to charity. That would make Robert see red. But there would be nothing the older brother could do about it. Nothing at all, no matter how big he got.

Gary dropped down at the large kitchen table and gazed out the darkened window at the night beyond. The only light came from down near the garage area and filled the old trees with a faint glow. Otherwise, the estate was dark and quiet.

His mother had made the entire family have breakfast together at this table every day. Gary had liked that, right up until the day she died. Robert, of course, had hated it, and complained every day about the chore.

And more often than not, he got hit by their father for his complaints. As far as Gary was concerned, Robert had usually deserved what he got. Granted, the old man had been hard on Robert when he was young, but the old man had been hard on everyone around him, including his own wife. The poor woman had died broken five years ago and it was on that day that Gary decided to take over the hard-earned and so-important business of his father and give every penny to charities, the very thing that his father would have hated. And his mother would have loved.

It had taken Gary almost two years before he convinced his father to change his will and give him that extra one percent. And not tell Robert he was doing so. Two years of being nice to an old man he hated.

Now the old man was dying. Gary knew his older brother wanted their father gone more than anything. For certain Robert would have been surprised to learn Gary did, also. Maybe even more than Robert.

Robert Service Sr.'s death would not be one that anyone would mourn. And that was a pity. No one should die that way.

Gary finished his milk and cookies and stood. He put the glass in the sink and then headed back for his father's room. His first inclination was to go see how his older brother was doing with his new growth and muscles, but after a moment, he decided that really didn't matter. What was important tonight was making sure the old man didn't change a thing in his will or his business until his death.

And to do that, Gary had to stay at his side and keep smiling.

There would be more than enough time for celebrating later, after the old man was dead.

The French Quarter in New Orleans is layered over and over with history. Every building, every courtyard, every park or street has a special history. The people who lived and worked in the French Quarter used that history to draw customers in any way they could. And it was also rumored that the streets and buildings of the French Quarter were filled with the ghosts of the people who had made all that history.

Remy LeBeau had never seen a ghost in all his years of growing up on those streets. And on this late night, he didn't expect to run into one. What he did expect was to discover who stood like a ghost in the shadows of a doorway across the street, listening to his private conversations.

Now one full hour had passed and Remy continued to stand, unmoving, in the shadows of the building where he had stepped after York left. He hadn't moved and neither had the person watching him across the narrow street.

Around Remy, the dark night of the French Quarter in New Orleans only flickered with life. At one point a young couple had walked past his position, not even noticing him. They had continued on past his watcher, also not noticing anything different on that side of the street.

A half dozen taxies had passed by, rushing through

the moist, damp air to get to drunken fares, most likely tourists who would be too drunk to realize until tomorrow morning that the cabbie had charged them five bucks too much. But the cab's lights hadn't illuminated Remy's watcher any more than Remy had allowed them to light him up.

One hour and it was still a draw. The guy was good, but Remy was better.

He waited for the moment when a cab had just passed his position, then stepped onto the sidewalk. Walking away at a normal pace, he turned the corner and started toward the lights and drunks of Bourbon Street three blocks away. He knew before he turned the corner that his shadow was following him.

Good.

Remy made sure he was far enough down the street for the guy watching him to get around the corner. Then slowly, as if he was just strolling, he turned into a small space between two buildings, actually a dark entrance to an interior courtyard, blocked three feet in by a high, vine-covered gate.

With two quick running bounds he was over the gate and into the courtyard beyond. Quickly he doubled back, moving silently through the shadows, so silently that he stepped over a sleeping cat at one point and didn't even wake the animal.

The courtyard was like an open plant-filled park in the center of the block, with dark windows fronting on it from all four directions. An old wooden staircase led up the side of one building and Remy headed up there, quickly gaining the roof of the three-story building and moving back toward the street.

He eased carefully and slowly up to the edge of the building and studied the street below. It took him only a moment to spot the guy who had been following him standing in a shadowed alcove across the street, watching the entrance Remy had entered.

Remy almost laughed aloud. Slowly he moved back from the edge, then quickly back down into the courtyard and out a door that lead back to the street they had started on. Then he went out and around a half block, coming up from behind the guy standing in the shadows.

"You lookin' for de men's room?" Remy asked, stepping in front of the guy. In his hand Remy had two playing cards. He could charge them and flick them before the guy could even turn, if he needed to.

"No," the man said, glancing at Remy without a hint of surprise or smile at the fact that he had been caught. "But I hear you are looking for Mr. Toole."

Remy studied the guy's face and eyes. He stood Remy's height, with pale, almost translucent blue skin that seemed to shine in the darkness of the street. His gaze was sharp, the dark black of his eyes almost painfully cold and unblinking.

"You hear good, *mon ami*," Remy said.

"Mr. Toole would be interested in meeting you, Mr. LeBeau. Please follow me."

Remy stepped back as the man moved forward. "Y'ask nice," Remy said, holding out his hand to stop the man, "but de answers come first."

However, what happened next was something Remy would have never suspected. His hand went right through the man's shoulder.

"What?" Remy said, jumping back, cards in his hand out in plain sight, charged, and ready to flip.

The man stopped, then laughed like a small barking dog, the sound bouncing off the nearby buildings.

"You have taken the fun out of the evening, Mr. LeBeau. That is too bad. I so enjoy a good evening."

With another laugh the man simply shimmered and then vanished.

Remy stood staring at the position the guy had been in a moment before, then glanced quickly around.

The streets of the French Quarter had returned to normal on this hot summer night. In the distance, a jazz band still blared out a tune. Cabs lined the curb two blocks up near Bourbon Street. The too-loud laughter of a drunk drifted over the buildings.

No one stood with Remy on that dark side street.

The guy had vanished.

More likely, he had never been on the street in the first place. Maybe it had been only a projection of some sort. It certainly hadn't been a ghost.

"Cute trick," Remy said aloud. "But de last laugh will be mine."

An hour later Remy could still not find the slightest trace of any projector or any other way the image of the man could have appeared on the streets of the French Quarter.

And every so often he thought he heard the sound of

a man laughing like a small barking dog. The sound gave him the chills, as if he were hearing a ghost laugh.

And it also made him mad. And Gambit was not a good person to make angry, even by a ghost.

CHAPTER 3

Slowly the sun broke over the edge of the deep valley, the light oozing down the rock and pine-covered hillside like someone had poured a bucket of thick, orange and yellow paint on the top of the ridge. It filled the cracks in the rocks and drove the morning mist higher into the air, where it swirled and then vanished.

Albert Jonathan had always loved sitting on the front porch of his small log cabin, watching the morning creep down into the deep Idaho valley he called home. For one hundred and sixty-three summers he had loved watching that sunrise. But this morning, for the first time, he dreaded the coming day.

Albert appeared, to the few who met him, to be the very picture of an Idaho mountain man. He had a long white beard and white hair. His face was rough and red from the sharp wind and bright sun. In the early years, he'd only worn animal skins, but since the turn of the century, and the first real gold mining rush into this area, he'd worn regular clothes, bought at the store a week's walk away in the little town of Yellow Pine. He only went into town once a year. He never talked to anyone and no one had paid him any attention. Fifty years back, he had reported to the authorities that Albert Jonathan had died and left his land to his son, Albert Jonathan Jr. He had no son, but the little ploy had covered the fact that he was living so long.

During the mining rush in the 1890s, he'd filed the first official homestead claim for his land and the eighty acres around it. During those early years he had been forced to defend it from all trespassers. There were three bodies buried down the hill a ways on a ridge overlooking the river. Back before the West got civilized, all three thought they could take his cabin and supplies.

The thought had gotten them all killed.

But mostly during the last eighty years the outside world had left him alone and for that he was glad. Since that very first trip into this wilderness area as a trapper in 1840, he had loved the steep mountains, the wild rivers, the unforgiving beauty of the Idaho back country, and he just wanted to live alone with that beauty for as many more years as he was going to live.

Five years after first trapping along the river that ran through this steep-walled valley, he had returned and built his first log cabin. He had been thirty-six and had fully expected to live out his last days trapping and doing a little mining, living alone in the mountains he loved.

He had not expected to live this long, not even after finding and picking up the large emerald that had cured his aching back, given him new teeth, and cleared up his fuzzy vision. But something about that large emerald had been very special, and for a long, long time he hadn't questioned it, only just lived and enjoyed, keeping the emerald tucked away in a very special hiding place.

But last night that had all changed.

He didn't know how he knew everything had changed, any more than he knew how he had lived for such a long time. But early last night he had felt another person crawl into his head with him, like an unwanted stranger entering a dark house.

An evil person.

And there was nothing Albert could do to kick this stranger out.

He knew that he was now connected to this evil force and it would soon come looking for him.

And for his stone. He knew that, too. The evil wanted the stone and to get the stone it had to kill Albert.

And like the three men down buried down on the ridge, it was going to get a fight.

No clouds broke the blue morning sky. The day was going to be hot and dry, as many summer days were in these mountains. Albert sat quietly watching the morning sun creep down the side of the valley wall, the Springfield .30–'06 rifle he'd bought in 1923 at his side. For a century and a half, Albert had lived in this valley and he knew every rock, every tree, every path and game trail in and out. And he could stand so still that even deer walked past him without knowing he was there.

He was a mountain man and these were his mountains. Mountain law would apply. He would defend his homestead.

Let the evil monster come. He would be ready.

Professor Charles Xavier sat alone in his study in the Xavier Institute for Higher Learning, waiting.

The stone fireplace crackled with a low fire even though the temperature in the Westchester area of New York was predicted to be in the high eighties. The Professor had discovered years before that a small fire took the chill off the marbled walls and hard floors of his study. He knew that the chill was mostly imagined, since his hoverchair covered his legs and kept him very comfortable. But for the most powerful telepath in the world, imagined comfort was almost as important as real.

Maybe even more so.

The Professor slumped slightly in his chair, his bald head reflecting the yellow flames of the fire in the dark room. Lately he'd come to like the study dark, even during the bright, summer days. Heavy drapes covered the tall windows and he never had them pulled open. The sameness of the dark study, day or night, kept him better focused on events outside the room. And lately there had been a lot of events.

It seemed there always were.

And now there was another.

Not as important on the scheme of things as some of the tasks his X-Men had handled lately, perhaps, but still one that needed to be dealt with.

There was a knock at the door and Scott Summers and Jean Grey entered. They both moved across the study to face the Professor as he turned around.

"You wanted to see us, sir," Scott said.

The Professor smiled. Scott had been with the team for a long time and he still sometimes acted like a young boy called into the principal's office when summoned. It was one of the countless things that the Professor liked about the leader of the X-Men.

"Yes," the Professor said, glancing down at his hoverchair, then back up at Scott, whose eyes were covered by sunglasses made of ruby quartz—the only material that could keep his powerful optic blasts in check. "There's a slight problem I need your help with."

"Anything," Jean said. At the moment she was dressed in a long red summer dress that accented her flowing red hair and pale skin. Scott wore light summer slacks and a Polo shirt. A tennis sweater was tied around his neck.

Jean and Scott made the perfect couple and always had, since their days as founding members of the X-Men—though the road from teammates to married couple was a rocky one. Still, even after everything they'd been through lately, all the missions and danger that being an X-Man meant, they looked rested and healthy. The two of them never ceased to amaze and please him.

"This item," the Professor said, "is sort of a family matter." He hesitated, then went on. "Cain is acting strangely again."

"'Acting strangely' how?" Scott asked.

"I'm not really sure," the Professor said. Cain Marko was the Juggernaut, and the X-Men had, so far, been the only thing that had managed to consistently stop or slow him down.

"I got this report faxed to me twenty minutes ago," the Professor said. He handed Scott a paper and waited for them to read it together.

Basically the fax said that the Juggernaut had stormed right through the middle of an Ohio town, heading east and slightly north. The problem was that he hadn't even bothered to use a road, simply walked through, or over, anything that was in front of him. So far, the damage had been minimal, and limited to vehicles, the occasional fire hydrant, and one deputy who made the mistake of trying to stop him and had a concussion to show for it. With the Juggernaut's strength, that could just as easily have been a broken neck.

"*Something* got under his helmet," Scott said, shaking his head. "That's for sure."

"You want us to confront him?" Jean asked.

The Professor nodded. "Yes. This is not a typical rampage, but the Juggernaut is still a danger. At the very least, we need to keep an eye on him."

"We'll handle it," Scott said confidently.

"Thank you, Scott," the Professor said.

"No problem, sir," Scott said.

Arm in arm, the two turned and left the dark study to return to the bright light of the summer day.

For a moment the Professor watched them go, then turned and stared into the fire.

There had been a number of times he wished he could get inside his stepbrother's mind to see what drove him. But the helmet he wore kept out any telepathic intrusion.

What are you up to, Cain?

There was no answer.

The plush office of Wingate Toole overlooked the river and parts of New Orleans beyond through two-inch-thick, bulletproof glass. A well-stocked bar filled the wall nearest the window with shelf after shelf of varied liqueurs and ornate glassware. The room was thickly carpeted and oak paneled, and the center of the area was dominated by a massive oak desk surrounded on three sides by heavy, high-backed chairs.

Air-conditioning kept the temperature of the room at exactly seventy-one degrees no matter how warm and humid it got outside. But this morning, to Wingate Toole, the temperature seemed much higher. The air felt thick and heavy with the fear that he held clamped inside his stomach. Every so often, during the morning, he had broken out into a thick, oily sweat.

A large man, built like a truck driver, Toole normally would be sitting at his desk at this time of the morning, his feet up, the smoke of his cigars filling the air as two or three of his business partners sat nearby talking over the coming day's activities.

But not this morning.

In the middle of the night, he'd sent his entire organization into full security alert. The warehouse complex that housed his office had become like Fort Knox.

No one got in or out.

Period.

Thick, steel shutters had been lowered over his huge office window, blocking the view and the rising sun. Extra machine guns had been set up facing every possible entrance. A helicopter circled slowly over the area, also armed and watching for any sign of anything different.

Over two hundred men with the newest, most modern and powerful weapons guarded the inside of the warehouse complex, all in full combat alert. All had orders to shoot to kill.

Toole chain-smoked cigars as he paced behind his desk. His most trusted associate, a tall, rail-thin man named Kyle, stood and watched, saying nothing. Kyle had been at Toole's side since shortly after the fear had crawled into Toole's head in the middle of the night and warned him of someone coming after him.

It had been a long night for both of them, but Toole knew it was only starting. The long night was going to stretch into days, maybe weeks, before this was finished. He knew it "inside" like he had known other things over the years that had helped him build this empire of crime.

And inside his head he kept hearing someone laughing.

Someone who wanted to come and take everything he had built.

He was not going to let that happen.

Not today, not ever.

It was time to check on one more detail.

Toole stopped pacing, yanked out his big leather chair, and dropped down into it. Stabbing his cigar out like he was crushing an insect with it, he glared up at Kyle. "Report to me every thirty minutes on the status of security around the building," Toole said. "Now get out of here."

Kyle only nodded and turned away.

Toole watched him go. It was Kyle's job to make sure no one could get in, and Toole trusted him to do it. And Kyle was very good at his job. Maybe even the best. But in this circumstance, Toole wanted to be informed all the time. After all, it was his life and his empire that was at risk.

Toole waited until Kyle snapped the door closed, then Toole flipped a switch, locking the door and electronically blocking all snooping devices. Then he sprang back to his feet and moved to the bar near the window. He could use a drink right about now, but didn't dare. He wouldn't drink until this was over.

In quick succession, he picked up and put down six different bottles on three shelves. As the last bottle was replaced, a slight click echoed through the large room and a small panel on the ornate wooden front of his desk opened wide.

Behind the panel was a small safe.

Toole moved three more bottles in succession, disarming an alarm system and explosive booby-trap that would instantly kill anyone who touched the safe while it was still activated.

Kneeling in front of the desk, he spun the dial to the correct combination and opened the safe, doing something he hadn't dared do all night.

Inside was a small leather pouch. He pulled it out and felt the reassuring weight inside.

As a construction worker doing a housing job outside of New Orleans, he'd stumbled on a large green stone buried in the mud. That day he'd been feeling hung over and a headache had been pounding at him for most of the hot afternoon. But the minute he touched the stone, his headache vanished and he felt stronger and more alive than he had in years.

He pocketed the stone without telling anyone and went back to work. A few days later, he started having ideas that got him thinking beyond just drinking and working construction. And since he'd touched the stone he felt great, had plenty of energy, and didn't much need sleep.

Five years later, he stood on the verge of taking over all of New Orleans.

He slid the gem out of the bag and held it in his hands. Normally, the feeling of strength he got from the stone would be enforced by touching it, and he had spent many a night just sitting at his desk holding the emerald.

But this time the touch of the stone was almost hot, and he dropped it at once.

Inside his head he heard the laughing again. And the words, *I'm coming.*

He picked the stone back up and put it in its pouch. He tossed it back into the safe and snapped the door shut, then closed the panel over it.

With a quick step back to the bar he armed the safe again.

Then, taking a deep breath he turned to the air and spoke to the voice in his head.

"Come and get me," Toole said, his voice muffled in the big room. "If you think you can."

The only reply was the faint impression of someone laughing.

Robert Service had spent the night sitting on the couch in his office, staring at the large emerald laying on the coffee table in front of him.

And laughing.

For some reason the joy of the emerald's power just

made him laugh. He'd never laughed much before, tending to take life more seriously, as his father had beat into him to do. But suddenly ending up with the power from the emerald had caused him to just laugh at the world and the wonderful luck he'd been handed by the man he hated.

How ironic it was.

And how funny.

After leaving his father and brother and returning to his office, he'd tried to sit at his desk, but his expanded frame had made the desk and all the chairs far too small for him. He had smashed a second chair simply by trying to sit in it. Obviously he'd have to have a special desk and chair made for him.

The couch had held him and he'd spent the night sitting there, staring at the emerald, alternately laughing at his good fortune and silently trying his best to get in touch with the feelings he had inside his head. Later in the day, he planned on testing some of the limits of his new size and strength, and having a doctor check him over to make sure he really was as healthy as he felt. But for the entire night he just sat and stared at the emerald.

And he got some answers.

His new physical power, even as great as it seemed, was only a small part of what it might be if he found the other two parts of the emerald. How he knew this, he had no idea. But, as with the strength, it just came with the emerald.

However, the emerald had given him no other special abilities that he could determine. He wasn't any smarter, that he could tell, and he couldn't sense anything that didn't directly relate to the emerald. And even then the sense was distant, like a whisper caught on a breeze.

But the whispers were loud enough for him to understand that two people possessed the other two emeralds. Both lived in the United States, one in the west, one in the south. Exactly where, he had no idea, nor did he know who the people were. But he could sense their presence and their direction and he figured that would be enough.

He could also sense another very powerful creature tied directly into the source of the energy of his emerald. Every time he thought of that creature, he felt a faint pain throughout his body and saw red. At the moment, he had no idea what that meant, but he assumed in time he would find out. What he did know was that the red creature was getting closer with every hour and the pain was increasing slightly.

He had no intention of being in this office when that creature, whatever it was, arrived.

A knock at his office door interrupted his musings over the emerald.

"Robert?" Gary's voice drifted faintly through the thick wooden door.

"Come in," Robert said, his voice booming so loud that it startled him. Glasses on the wet bar shook from the intensity of it. It was going to take some time to get used to his new power.

The door slowly opened and Gary stepped through, his face pale, his eyes sunken from lack of sleep. But at the sight of Robert, Gary's face got even paler and his eyes widened with the shock of what he was seeing.

Robert laughed, again rocking the glasses on the bar

across the room. "Gonna take some getting used to, isn't it, *little* brother?"

Gary nodded and stopped in the doorway, still staring at the mostly nude body of Robert.

Robert's shredded clothes had fallen away during the night and he'd covered himself with a blanket that looked more like a towel over his huge body. He knew exactly how he looked—he'd spent a considerable amount of time staring into the mirror—and he liked it. He liked the size of his chest and arms more than anything.

After a moment Gary asked, "Are you all right?"

"Better than ever," Robert said, standing and wrapping the blanket around his waist like a beach towel. His head almost reached the tall ceiling.

Gary's mouth actually opened in shock as Robert stood and faced him, and it was clear to Robert that the look in Gary's eyes was pure fear.

"Jealous, little brother?" Robert asked, and laughed.

Gary shook his head slowly, never taking his eyes off Robert. "Just worried," he said softly.

"You," Robert said, pointing at Gary, "worried about *me*? Now that's a funny one."

"You *are* my brother," Gary said.

Robert stepped one large, building-shaking step closer to Gary and the smaller man cowered back slightly, but, to his credit, didn't budge.

"Are we lucky? Has the old man gone to meet the devil yet?" Robert asked.

Gary shook his head. "Keep your voice down," he said. "He'll hear you."

Robert laughed even harder at that. "And you think

I care?'' Robert asked. Then he glared down at Gary. ''You just keep sniveling around Father like you've been doing and leave me alone. I've got a few trips to make and I may be gone for a few days. Call me if the old man croaks.''

Gary said nothing, but simply turned and left, slamming the door as he went.

Robert laughed, long and hard. He knew his laughs were echoing through the big, old mansion. He just hoped they were driving his brother and father crazy. It would be an added benefit to this wonderful new strength and size.

Too bad he couldn't stay around longer and have even more fun with them. Maybe after he found the other parts of the emerald and returned, there would be time.

''Oh, that would be fun,'' he said, and laughed again.

Gary let the booming, echoing laughs of his brother follow him down the gloomy halls of the mansion. Robert's size was incredible. During the night Gary had almost convinced himself that he'd imagined what had happened with the emerald and Robert. But now, in the light of day, it was clear that Robert's new size and power were very real.

That made his plans even harder. Robert was just crazy enough that he'd kill his own brother when he found out how he had been tricked out of control of the Service businesses. And now Robert had the power to do it.

There had to be a way to get Robert back to normal, or at least a way to control him.

Gary headed toward his father's room. Maybe the old man knew a way. After all, he'd been the one to find the emerald in the first place.

Last night, after Robert had touched the emerald, their father had had a very mild heart attack. The nurse had kept him sedated for the remainder of the night, and a doctor had checked him over this morning. No change. He was going to die shortly of cancer, if his heart didn't take him first. And there wasn't a thing medical science could do to stop it.

And for that Gary was glad.

As Gary got to his father's room, the old man was starting to come around again.

The machines near his bed were all active and the heart monitor beeped continuously. The morning nurse, a middle-aged, brown-haired woman with hard gray eyes sat on a chair near the machines, reading a Stephen King novel.

Gary let the smell of the cancer envelop him as he entered the room. Even after being so close to his father over the last month as the cancer got worse, the smell still turned his stomach. He doubted if he'd ever clear that smell out of his memory.

"Father," Gary said, moving over beside the blinking old man and sitting down in his normal chair beside the bed. "Go slow. I'm right here."

But the old man seemed upset. He grabbed Gary's arm with a surprisingly strong grip, pulled himself up slightly, and looked Gary right in the eye.

"Did I dream it?" he asked, his voice hard and raspy. "Did Robert touch the emerald?"

"I'm afraid he did," Gary said.

The old man let go of Gary's arm and sank back, closing his eyes with a sigh.

The beeping of the machine increased and the nurse looked up at it, then went back to reading.

"Nurse," Gary said, "Could we possibly have a moment alone, please?"

The woman glanced at the machines, nodded, then stood and left the room without a word, closing the door behind her as she went.

"Father," Gary said, lightly touching the back of the old man's hand. "Tell me more about the emerald. Is there any way to return Robert to normal?"

The old man shook his head, flopping it back and forth as if he were having a nightmare. Then he stopped and opened his eyes again. "All I know is what that monk told us," he said. "And I told you all he said last night."

"Oh," Gary said, sitting back in his chair, dejected. So much for getting a quick fix from the old man.

"But," his father said softly, almost as if he were afraid to speak.

Gary sat back up straight and again touched his father's hand. "But what, father?"

"In my desk," he said. "Right-hand drawer in a file labeled research, there is a picture cut out of a newspaper. It's near the back of the file."

"And what's the picture of?" Gary asked.

"A creature," his father said.

Gary shook his head in frustration. "Why will it help?" Gary asked. "What creature?"

His father opened his eyes wide and stared at Gary.

THE JEWELS OF CYTTORAK

"A creature who walks today and who looks like . . ."

"Cyttorak?"

"No. That's not what the creature in the newspaper was called," the old man said. He weakly waved a hand. "Go. Look."

Gary nodded. "I'll be back shortly," he said.

On the way out he motioned for the nurse to go back inside, then at a quick pace he headed for his father's office near the front of the mansion.

The place hadn't even been cleaned much since his father turned ill. The old man hadn't wanted it touched. And since both Gary and Richard had their own offices in other areas of the mansion, it hadn't mattered.

The file was right where the old man said it would be, and the clipping was toward the back of the file. The minute Gary saw the newspaper article he dropped back into the tall desk chair his father had used for years. His heart was racing and he couldn't seem to catch his breath.

"Oh, no," he said softly.

The picture on yellowed newspaper was of a giant human wearing armor and a bullet-like helmet, giving him the appearance of having no neck. Richard was nowhere near the size of the guy in the picture, but his body was clearly shaping in that direction.

Under the picture the caption read: JUGGERNAUT ON RAMPAGE AGAIN.

CHAPTER 4

emy had spent most of the hot, humid New Orleans summer day sitting in the shade of an umbrella on the edge of a courtyard café, sipping iced tea and waiting.

His headband kept the sweat out of his face and his hair up and out of his eyes. His Gambit costume under his duster wasn't as hot as he'd expected it to be in these conditions, which was a relief, considering that the duster did nothing to keep him cool. And wearing the duster had got him some puzzled looks. He'd just stared right back until the person staring looked away. After all, it was his business if he wanted to sit and cook, wasn't it?

He sipped on the iced tea and stared at a group entering the café. Nothing. He knew who he was waiting for and by now he assumed that person knew he was waiting. In New Orleans, nothing stayed hidden for long.

And he wasn't hiding by any means, so eventually his target would show.

He just hoped it was before he died of heat exhaustion.

He had obviously spent too many years up north with the Professor and the X-Men. New Orleans was his hometown, the place he loved more than anything, yet he had forgotten just how hot and humid the city could get. He figured his not remembering was like a lover not noticing an imperfection in a partner.

Suddenly behind him, Remy could sense a movement, a slight rustling of the bushes that formed a row along the inside of the courtyard, as if a slight wind had brushed them. But the day was calm and the air thick and unmoving. And he had sat where he could watch all entrances, and no one had moved around behind him from the courtyard.

That meant that only another thief could be there, and a good one at that. And only one, besides himself, was that good, which meant his hoped-for guest had finally arrived.

"Sit, *mon ami*," Remy said, not turning around, but indicating the empty chair beside him. He took another drink as beside him a figure pulled out a chair and sat down.

"I see you're as good as always, LeBeau," the thin, white-shirted figure said, sitting down and motioning for a waiter to bring him a tea.

Remy tipped his glass in a gesture of thanks at the compliment, then smiled at his friend, Claude deMont. "A very long time."

And it had been a long time since LeBeau had last seen his childhood friend. The last time had been under very bad circumstances as Remy fought to get Bella, his wife, the elixir of life to save her. He had succeeded in saving her, but in the process had him several enemies. And with Bella not remembering him, the pain of the price he paid haunted him like a hunger that wouldn't go away no matter how much he ate.

But since Claude had decided to join him, it appeared Claude was not one of those enemies.

The waiter served the iced tea to Claude, refilled

Remy's glass, and left. For a moment they both sat silently, staring at the courtyard.

Then Claude spoke softly. "If I knew you were here, so does Bella."

"De risks," Remy said, and shrugged. "Worth it to see my ol' friend."

Claude shook his head slowly in amusement. Over the years he had done a lot of laughing at the risks Remy had taken. And Claude had shaken his head in amazement at what Remy had managed to accomplish. To Remy, it was always fun to amaze his old friend.

And this time Remy knew why Claude had such a reaction. Bella had become the leader recently of the Assassins Guild, the deadly enemies of thieves like Remy. And it seemed that Remy was at the top of her list.

"Besides," Remy said, "Bella has herself some bigger problems den me."

"Toole?" Claude said, letting the surprise come through in his voice. "You know?"

Remy only nodded.

Claude took another drink and then leaned forward slightly over the table. "Toole's messin' it all up, LeBeau. It's like the old ways mean nothin'."

"And de guilds can't take him down, *hahn*?"

"Can't get to him," Claude said.

"Well," Remy said, sipping on his iced tea. "Maybe it de time for someone to talk to de guy."

Claude nodded. "Past time."

"So?" Remy said, glancing over at Claude.

Claude sighed, then glanced around the courtyard

while pretending to drink. Then he sat his glass down and told Remy what he wanted to hear.

"The old French Imports warehouse complex down on the river," Claude said as if he was just talking about the weather. "It's defended better than any military complex I've ever seen. None of us have managed to get inside. Two have died trying."

Remy just nodded, then sipped on his tea.

Claude downed the rest of his tea and stood. "Good luck, LeBeau."

"*Merci beaucoup, mon ami,*" Remy said.

Claude moved quickly across the courtyard and out onto the street beyond.

After a moment Remy stood and followed, moving slowly, as if he didn't have a care in the world. Underneath, all he wanted to do was get out of the sun, into a cool room, and wait for the night to arrive.

But he didn't dare hurry.

At this moment, after sitting out in the open as long as he had, there were just too many risks. Before he could get into that cool room, he had to disappear and make absolutely sure no one was following.

It took him almost an hour.

One very long, very hot, hour.

Scott Summers, having changed into the blue-and-yellow uniform that identified him as Cyclops, co-leader of the X-Men, eased the *Blackbird* upward until it hovered above its pad behind the Xavier mansion. Then he turned it west and sent it forward, heading for the Juggernaut's last known position.

The Professor's stepbrother had been one of their greatest problems over the years, and today might be another of those fights that none of them seemed to win against Juggernaut. Scott sincerely hoped not.

"I'll agree with you there," Jean said from the co-pilot seat beside him, smiling.

The beautiful Phoenix had read his thoughts.

Scott smiled back at his wife as he eased the speed of the X-Men's plane upward. He and Jean were so connected, in so many ways, that their thoughts were linked by Jean's power almost automatically. He liked it that way, and he knew she did, too. There were many times over the years that the link between them had saved their lives.

She reached across and rested her hand on his arm, letting the physical touch add to the mental. With Jean at his side, he felt whole.

Again Scott smiled at her, then returned his thoughts to the mission ahead.

Behind them, in the right seat, was Dr. Henry McCoy—Hank to his friends, the Beast to the general public. The blue-furred Hank had been spending days, and nights lately, wrapped up in his lab, working frantically to find a cure for the deadly Legacy Virus, a virus that had been introduced into the world by the madman Stryfe. It primarily attacked mutants, but had recently spread into the human population. Hank had redoubled his efforts of late, following the death of a young boy named Walter Nowland, who had died at the Xavier Institute's sister school,

Xavier's School for Gifted Youngsters in Massachusetts.

But so far, even the brilliance of the smartest X-Man couldn't crack the cure. And the frustration was driving the doctor to slamming his fist against things, not a typical gesture for him.

So when this opportunity to check up on the Juggernaut came along, Scott figured it would be a good time to get Hank some air. Let the good doctor's nerves recharge a little. And against the Juggernaut, it never hurt to have Hank along.

Hank hadn't exactly been pleased with the interruption, but he hadn't really objected that hard, either. It seemed he knew that Scott was right.

Behind Scott sat Rogue, the fourth X-Man on the flight. She wore her brown flight jacket over her green-and-yellow X-Men uniform. She'd brushed her hair back and upward, making the white streak in her auburn hair even more prominent. As the plane climbed and leveled off she just stared out the side window, her attention clearly miles away.

And Scott knew why. Since Gambit had left for New Orleans, she'd been feeling lost. When Jean mentioned the flight to check up on the Juggernaut, she'd volunteered to go along. Anything to keep her mind a little busy and off of her feelings for the Cajun.

But at the moment it didn't look as if it was working.

"Well," Scott said, "this shouldn't take long. Last report had Juggernaut crossing the border into New York about halfway up the state line."

"Any idea what set the big guy off this time?" Rogue asked, still staring out at the passing green valleys.

"Nothing," Jean said.

"Based on our experiences with Mr. Marko," Hank said, "it would take little, if any, outside stimulus to precipitate an event of this nature."

"Well," Scott said, turning the *Blackbird* slightly downward toward the farms and rolling hills of central New York, "he isn't exactly covering his tracks." Scott pointed ahead.

"Oh my stars and garters," Hank said, leaning forward slightly to see past Jean's shoulder.

Scott agreed.

A white, two-story farm house had been knocked down completely and there was a Juggernaut-sized hole in the side of a nearby red barn. A small stand of trees had a path knocked down through them beyond the barn. Scott just hoped the family in the house was all right.

"Me, too," Jean said, reading his thoughts. "I'll see if I can find out."

As Scott turned the *Blackbird* slightly to follow the line of destruction, Jean stared out the window at the farmhouse, taking in the thoughts of those below. After a moment she sighed and said, "They're all alive," she said. "And very angry."

"They got a right to be angry," Rogue said, staring back at the destruction the Juggernaut had caused. "He's destroyed their home."

"There he is," Scott said.

Ahead of them the Juggernaut pounded one foot in front of another across an open field, taking giant, distance-eating strides. It was amazing to Scott how fast he could travel on the ground. The Juggernaut never tired and never stopped for anything, basically moving as the crow flies, only on the ground.

The problem was that he went over or through anything in his way.

"I would recommend not landing the *Blackbird* in his path," Hank said. "It might not be a propitious location for the health of our transportation."

"Agreed," Scott said, swinging the *Blackbird* in a high arc over Juggernaut and landing the plane softly a good half a mile ahead and off to one side of the behemoth's path.

"We're not to engage him right away," Scott said. "We'll try to talk to him first. Jean, you and I will pace him to his right. Rogue, you take Hank and stay with him on his left."

"Understood," Hank said.

Rogue nodded.

"Let's go, X-Men," Scott said.

Without another word they climbed out of the *Blackbird* and took up positions facing the unstoppable Juggernaut heading their way.

It had taken Robert Service Jr. most of the morning to get some clothes his new size ordered, then delivered to the estate. His proportions had completely changed—not just six inches of height but considerably more bulk. It had cost a great deal to have it done, but he didn't have much choice at the moment. He needed the clothes. And he had the money.

About twenty minutes after Gary had left, Robert suddenly felt as if he didn't have much time. The big, red creature was getting closer and the pain was growing slightly. He needed to get out of there, head west, find the second part of the emerald. It was like an aching need and he really had no desire to deny the drive.

Nor any reason to.

He strode across the grounds of his family estate and into the hangar beside the private runway, enjoying the speed his new stride and power gave him. He bet there were many things about being this powerful he was going to enjoy.

"Is the plane ready?" he said as he entered the large hanger. His voice boomed over the metal and concrete like a thunderclap.

The two pilots of the private jet jumped to their feet from positions in a small lounge. They both just stared at him, fear slowly filling their eyes.

"Sorry, gentlemen," he said, lowering his voice to what seemed to be a whisper to his ears. "Still not used to the new lungs."

The pilot, a thin, graying man by the name of Harold Trimble, had been working for the Service family for almost ten years. He was the first to finally get his voice after swallowing twice. "What happened to you?"

"Just a little growth hormone," Robert said, and laughed. Again his voice boomed around the hanger and the two men's eyes widened. The young copilot actually took a step back and looked like he wanted to run.

"Sorry," Robert said, whispering. "I'll get the hang of this new voice sooner or later."

Both men just nodded, but Robert could tell they didn't look any less afraid of him. And that was just fine, as far as he was concerned. It never hurt to have employees afraid of their boss. Robert figured it added an extra level of work and care to an employee's performance.

"Is the plane ready?"

Harold nodded slowly. "Yes, sir."

"Good," Robert whispered. "Let's get in the air. And just head west, say for San Francisco. I'll tell you along the way if we need to change directions."

Harold and the young copilot both nodded.

Robert turned and climbed into the jet, barely fitting in the seat. He finally managed to find a comfortable position on the large leather couch. After all this was settled and his father was dead, he'd have to get a larger plane. This one just wouldn't do for a man of his size.

And power.

With the last thought he once again laughed softly to himself.

Cain Marko's chest still hurt, but the closer he got to upper New York State, the better it felt. It was as if the pain was dragging him there like he was nothing more than a stupid homing pigeon. As a kid he had hated to be bossed around. Now that he was the Juggernaut, he was powerful enough that no one could do that to him anymore. But now the pain in his chest was like a nagging boss, forcing him onward. And the farther he went, the angrier he got.

THE JEWELS OF CYTTORAK

Whatever was causing this pain was going to be real sorry, real soon. He hadn't been this mad in years.

The roar of the X-Men's plane over his head distracted him. *That's all I need now*, he thought, *my step-brother's students buzzing around me like flies, doing their do-gooder deeds*. Most likely they were going to try to stop him.

That just wasn't going to happen.

The X-Men's plane landed off to one side of his path up ahead.

Four X-Men climbed out and Cain recognized them as Cyclops, Phoenix, Rogue, and the Beast. The latter two moved to a safe distance to the right of his path and stood waiting.

On the other side of his path Summers and Grey floated side by side.

Fine. Let them just float there. He wasn't stopping for them now or any time in the future. He'd just walk right between them and take their best shots and keep going. At the moment they weren't even worth his time.

But as he went between them they surprised him. They simply floated along beside him, pacing his speed across the empty field.

"What's the matter?" he asked, turning to look at the pair without stopping. "Nothing better to do on a hot summer day than bother a man on his own business?"

"Actually, Cain," Summers said, "just wondering why you're tearing up all this real estate."

"Taking a train would clearly be less taxing," McCoy said from the other side of Cain. "And far less damaging to the local flora."

Cain glared at the blue ball of fur and simply got a shrug and a smile in return.

"Look," Cain said, turning his head to look at Summers without missing a step on his journey, "just leave me alone. I got something I need to do and you and that creepy stepbrother of mine can't help me or stop me. All right?"

"Fine by us," Summers said. "But just tell us why the hurry and all the destruction?"

Cain snorted. "You really want to know, one-eye? It's because something up ahead of me there is causing me pain. And I don't much like pain."

"Two aspirins seem to work on most pains," McCoy said.

Cain took a swipe at him without breaking stride, but missed.

Suddenly the pain in his chest grew worse, in a way he'd come to know meant he was going in the wrong direction.

"What?" he said aloud. He stopped and turned slightly to the north.

No change. The pain remained.

"Cain?" Summers said, floating off to one side with Grey. "What happened?"

"Would you stop your yapping for a minute," Cain said. "Give me a chance to figure this out."

Thankfully they did as he asked.

He turned slightly south. Again no change in the pain radiating in his chest.

He turned farther south. Nothing.

Then even farther, so that he was facing slightly west.

And the pain seemed lighter.

He turned all the way around to the west and the pain lightened. Either he had passed what was causing him pain, or it had changed position, going west of where he now stood.

He growled real low in his throat, then started back in the direction he'd just came. The thing causing him this pain was going to pay, and pay good. And it couldn't run forever. At some point he'd catch up to it.

"Cain?" Summers said. "What just happened?"

But Cain said nothing, only put his head down and headed west, ignoring whatever got in his way.

CHAPTER 5

The rolling hills, trees, and farms gave the central New York area a feeling of serenity most summer afternoons. Light breezes swirled the humid afternoon air, giving farmers reasons to keep windows open for a hope of that slight, windy comfort.

But on this summer afternoon there was a path of destruction into those peaceful fields. A path that had gone only so far and then suddenly stopped.

Four X-Men stood in the open field at the point where the Juggernaut had just suddenly turned around, watching as he stomped off west, following his own tracks back in the direction he'd come.

Phoenix watched him go, wishing more than ever that she could read the Juggernaut's thoughts. Just for an instant, just to get a clue as to what was driving him. But his helmet effectively blocked any attempts she made, making her feel as if she were staring at a blank wall inside her head every time she tried.

"What was that all about?" Rogue asked.

"Worst case of decision-interruptus I have ever seen," Hank said.

Scott shook his head. "Rogue, keep an eye on his path ahead, make sure there isn't anything else in his path that might cause problems if he decides to plow through it."

"Right, boss," she said. "Back in a jiff."

She waved at the Juggernaut as she went over him, then sped off in a green-and-yellow streak.

The Juggernaut paid her no attention at all, simply kept walking, one pounding step after another.

"I'll report to the Professor," Jean said to Scott and Hank. "Tell him what happened."

Scott only nodded.

Professor? She focused on Charles Xavier and his dark study, blocking out the warm afternoon around her and sending her thoughts to him.

Yes, Jean. The Professor's voice came back clear and strong inside her mind. *I can read from your thoughts what happened. I, too, am baffled as to the cause.*

Should we just follow him for the moment, maybe talk to him again?

Yes, the Professor said. *But do not engage him unless you need to do so to save lives. As long as he is content to simply walk, we will minimize the ancillary effects. Engaging him will only result in much greater damage.*

Understood.

The Professor broke the link in Jean's mind, leaving a slightly empty sense for a brief instant.

She turned to Scott and for Hank's sake spoke aloud. "The Professor wants us to follow Cain, but not try to stop him unless lives are at stake. And if we can, talk to him again."

Scott nodded. "All right. We'll go as soon as Rogue returns."

"If you don't mind," Hank said, "I'll wait in the *Blackbird* with the air conditioning turned up." He plucked at a long patch of blue fir. "Not the best outfit for this weather, you understand."

THE JEWELS OF CYTTORAK

• • •

Gary Service had spent the afternoon in the coolness of his office, staring at his computer, studying everything he could find about the Juggernaut in any online reference he could think of.

In one account, he discovered that the Juggernaut's power supposedly came from a large ruby, but the author of the article didn't know for sure. And the author had no idea where the ruby had come from, or how it gave the Juggernaut his power. Only pointless speculation.

Another article studied the Juggernaut's powers and abilities from some of the fights he'd been seen in. That article basically came to the conclusion that the man was unstoppable by just about anyone, and anything, on the planet.

A third article gave the Juggernaut's real name, Cain Marko, and that he was stepbrother to the renowned geneticist, Charles Xavier. There were lots of pictures in all the articles, mostly with the Juggernaut fighting against some team called the X-Men or another, and a couple against Spider-Man. But nowhere, in any of the articles, did it mention any weaknesses. In fact, the most common word used to describe him was *unstoppable*.

Gary finally gave up, signed off, and headed to the kitchen for some early dinner. His eyes were tired and his back ached from sitting and staring at the computer screen for the entire afternoon.

If Robert became a second Juggernaut, unstoppable by even powerful mutants like the X-Men, there would be nothing Gary could do. All his years of planning, of being nice to the old man, would be wasted.

There had to be a way to get Robert back to normal.

It wasn't until thirty minutes later, after the cook had fixed him a turkey sandwich, a salad, and a large iced tea, that Gary remembered the reference to Charles Xavier.

"Hadn't thought of that," Gary said aloud as he sat and stared out over the manicured lawns of the estate, watching the red fill the sky from a beautiful sunset.

Maybe the Juggernaut's stepbrother could help Gary with Robert. Maybe this Xavier person knew something about what happened to Marko and could help Gary stop the same thing from happening to Robert?

Maybe . . .

It was the only thought Gary had at the moment. And doing something was better than sitting there at the kitchen counter watching the sun set on the day and on his plan to control his father's business.

Gary took the sandwich and iced tea back to his office and sat at his desk. After another quick search back on the Internet, he found a reference to the Xavier Institute for Higher Learning, run by Professor Charles Xavier, in Salem Center, New York. He wasn't even that far away.

Signing off, Gary then called directory assistance for Westchester County. A moment later the operator gave him the Institute's number.

Robert Service slept for what felt like only an hour, slumped on the leather couch, as the private jet crossed the country. He hadn't slept a wink the night before and hadn't even felt tired, but shortly after the plane lifted off he grew sleepy and dozed off, answering the question he had wondered about the night before: Would touching the emerald mean he didn't need to sleep any more? The answer was clearly no.

As he awoke, he realized the light in the cabin had a slight reddish tint to it. A quick glance out the window told him the red came from the sun being low in the sky in front of them, shining light through a thin layer of high clouds. He'd obviously slept much longer than he had first thought.

He punched the pilot intercom button. "Where are we?"

A moment later the pilot's voice came back. "Approaching the Reno area, sir. We should be in San Francisco in thirty to forty minutes."

"Thank you," he said, easing back as best he could with his huge bulk on the small couch. He took a few deep breaths to clear the sleep from his mind, then tried to focus on the direction of the other stones.

Nothing came to him. It was as if they'd both simply vanished from his mind.

Quickly, trying not to panic, he opened the small case he'd carried aboard and dug down into a small, hidden pocket below his bathroom kit. He quickly pulled out the small pouch that held the emerald and opened it, sliding the emerald onto the palm of his hand.

It was like an old friend coming home.

He could feel the energy from the emerald clearing away the sleep, flooding through his body like an electrical circuit recharging a battery.

And the other parts of the stones again called to him in the back of his mind, like lost children begging to be rescued.

He laughed again, as he had last night. The feeling of power was just so wonderful, like having a good meal, a good drink, and a night with a beautiful woman all wrapped into one moment of feeling.

Then he realized something had changed. The western part of the emerald was no longer west, but now north. They had flown too far.

He punched the pilot's intercom button. "Turn north."

"Sir," the pilot said after a long moment. "We're going to need fuel shortly. We've only got another two hundred miles in our safety limit."

"Understood," Robert said, keeping his voice low so it didn't echo in the small cabin of the jet. "Can you reach Boise safely?"

Again a slight pause. "Yes, sir."

"Good," Robert said. "Refuel there."

"Yes, sir," the pilot said.

A few moments later the jet did a slow banking turn to the north.

Inside Robert's head the feeling was right again.

And the power flowed through the emerald and into his body, making him again laugh at the sheer joy of it.

The low fire crackled in the fireplace, sending an occasional spark up the stone chimney. The faint smell of wood smoke always filled the dark study and the Professor liked it that way. He knew the sun was setting beyond the heavy drapes of his office. He knew the evening would be a warm one, perfect for floating in his chair out onto the back lawn to watch the stars come out.

But that kind of resting and enjoying of life was not something he felt he could take the time for at the moment. The problems of his team, and mutants in the world in general, were taking more and more of his time and energy. And he never seemed to have enough of either to begin to match the problems.

And now Cain was on a rampage again. He shook his head and stared into the fire. *Why now?* he wondered.

The Professor wished he knew, but Cain was not one to do much talking, and especially not to him. Cain had hated him since they were teenagers, since he thought his father paid more attention to Charles than him. And he might have been right, to a degree. But Cain had been a hard child, wild and mean, made that way by beatings at the hands of his father.

And when an accidental fire killed his father, Cain managed to blame it on Charles and the hatred grew into something they would never clear up. But Cain was still his brother and Charles was never going to feel totally free of the responsibility.

The Professor checked his watch. Three hours had passed since Cain had suddenly changed directions and he showed no signs of stopping. What was driving him? Something was, of that there was no doubt. And the only hope they had of stopping his rampage was to find the cause.

There was a knock at the door and Bishop, one of the

more recent additions to the X-Men, stuck his head into the dark office, looking slightly worried.

"Yes, Bishop," the Professor said. He could have probed the big man's mind easily, but he had learned a long time ago to honor the boundaries of other's thoughts. They were personal things and unless it was an emergency, he never so probed without permission.

"There is a person on the phone by the name of Gary Service who says he must speak to you urgently regarding the Juggernaut."

The Professor was about to tell Bishop to take the man's name and number, but at the mention of the Juggernaut he nodded.

"Thank you," the Professor said, floating in his hoverchair toward his desk and the phone. "I'll speak to him."

More than likely it was just one of Cain's poor victims who had a house, or some other property, destroyed, looking for some kind of compensation. A few of Cain's victims had tried to sue the Professor for the Juggernaut's damages, but it had never held up. He was not responsible for Cain's actions, even though at times he felt he was.

"Charles Xavier," the Professor said.

"Yes, Dr. Xavier," the agitated voice on the other end of the line said. "My name is Gary Service. And I'm looking for a little help, or information."

"I'm not sure about my ability to help, Mr. Service," the Professor said calmly. "But I can certainly listen to your question."

"Thank you, sir," Service said.

The Professor heard him take a deep breath, most likely to calm his nerves.

"I understand," Service said, "that you are the step-brother of Cain Marko, also known as the Juggernaut. Is that right?"

"That is correct," the Professor said, waiting for Service to get to his question.

"And the Juggernaut's power comes from a ruby," Service said. "Is that correct?"

"In a manner of speaking," the Professor said. That question had him puzzled. "The ruby is like a pipe that directs the power to the Juggernaut from another plane."

"Okay . . ." Service said, letting the word trail off, clearly not understanding. Then he took another deep, loud breath, then rushed into his question. "Is there any way of reversing the effects the gem has on the Juggernaut?"

Service's question actually shocked the Professor. It certainly was not what he had been expecting. "There is no method, that has been brought to my attention, to reverse the effects. I guarantee you, sir, that if there was, someone would have used it on my stepbrother years ago."

"I was afraid of that," Service said. It sounded as if all the air and energy had simply gone out of the man. Where a moment before his voice had been high and worried, now it suddenly sounded like he was about to give up living.

"Sir," the Professor said. "What is your interest in all this?"

Service sighed, then laughed softly. "I suppose it won't hurt to tell anyone now. It's pretty obvious just looking at him."

"At the beginning, Mr. Service. Please start at the beginning." As he spoke, the Professor glanced down at the caller ID display on the phone, which gave him the general location from which Service was calling, based on the area code.

"Last night my dying father showed my brother Robert and me a large emerald he said he found in an old stone temple in Korea. You're not going to believe the next part," Service said, laughing half-heartedly to himself. "I saw it, I was there, and I still don't believe it."

"You would be amazed at what I will believe," the Professor said. He turned his powerful mind outward, searching for thought patterns that matched Service's conversation. Often one's surface thoughts related directly to what one was saying, so isolating Service's mind would be comparatively easy as long as the Professor continued talking to him.

"My brother," Service said, "is an egotistical, power-hungry man. My father had never touched the emerald because he said a monk had warned him not to. But my brother ignored him and picked it up."

"And what happened then?" the Professor asked, finally locating the mind of Gary Service. He began a simple surface probe, not wanting to go too deeply. He just scanned enough to see if the man spoke the truth.

"Robert simply changed, grew, maybe six inches taller, and much, much bigger." Service laughed. "I told you that you wouldn't believe me."

"Oh," the Professor said, "I believe you." Service's own thoughts confirmed what he saw. Indeed, the image of the enlarged Robert Service lay foremost in the man's mind. "There is a ruby that turned my stepbrother into the Juggernaut. It would be logical then, that there might be another gemstone of similar power. Did the gem attach itself in any way to your brother?"

"No," Service said. "Robert was still holding it in his hand and laughing when he left the room. Why?"

"To be honest, Mr. Service, I don't know. But it may mean the transformation is not complete. We can only hope. Where is your brother now?"

"He flew out of here this afternoon in our private jet. He didn't say where he was headed, but it wouldn't be hard to track, since he's in the family plane."

"And just where are you?" the Professor asked.

"About a hundred miles north of you."

The Professor nodded to himself. A piece of the puzzle had just fallen into place. Cain had been headed for the Service estate. Somehow, in some way, the ruby that gave Cain his power must be hooked up to the emerald Service touched. And when Robert Service left, he took the stone with him, causing Cain to stop and follow Robert Service back west.

But why was Robert Service going west right after touching the stone? What did he need out there?

"Dr. Xavier?" Gary Service said. "Are you still there?"

"Yes," the Professor said. "I'm sorry." He thought a moment, then probed Service a bit more deeply. He did not like doing so, but it was necessary to preserve the X-Men's secrets. The general public did not know that Charles Xavier, renowned authority on mutants, was the mentor of the X-Men, nor that he was a mutant himself.

Fortunately, Gary Service's awareness of the X-Men was limited to the fact of their existence. He had no idea of the current roster. The Professor could use that to his advantage.

"As it happens, you are the second call I've gotten today regarding my stepbrother. Are you familiar with Dr. Henry McCoy?"

"The blue-furred scientist, yes?" Service said after a moment. "Used to be with the Avengers or the Fantastic Four or somesuch."

"The Avengers," the Professor clarified. Hank had, in fact, served a lengthy tenure with Earth's Mightiest Heroes. "He still helps them occasionally, and he and some others have been monitoring the Juggernaut's recent movements. When next he checks in, would you object if I put him in touch with you?"

"Certainly," Gary Service said, the energy and hope returning clearly to his voice. "The Avengers stopped dozens of threats in the past. Perhaps they can stop my brother, too."

"Excellent," the Professor said, and got the exact address for the Service estate.

"Thank you, Dr. Xavier."

"No," the Professor said. "I think I need to be thanking you for calling me. And let's hope we can help your brother before he becomes like Cain."

"I hope so, too," Service said.

The Professor hung up the phone and turned to stare into the low fire. Gary Service had answered a few questions, but had raised a great many more. And the possibility of two Juggernaut-like creatures roaming this planet made the Professor shudder, even in the warm room.

As the sun set, the tourists and party life took over the warm, humid streets of the French Quarter like a wall of soldiers suddenly ordered to charge the enemy. The conflicting sounds of a dozen jazz and blues bands fought for attention up and down Bourbon Street from open cafés and smoke-filled bars. Tourists pushed and laughed and walked, all fighting the battle to have a good time in a city known for good times.

The heat of the day still smothered the streets of the Quarter and the smells of human sweat mixed with smoke and open-air cooking. The restaurants all over the Quarter were filled to capacity with customers and the wonderful aroma of Cajun cooking drifted in and out of the shadows like a phantom, grabbing hungry people in a seductive, addictive embrace.

Remy LeBeau paid no attention to the crowds or the wonderful smells filling the tight sidewalks and spilling out into the narrow streets. He stood silently, tucked back in the shadow of a deep doorway, watching the street where the night before his "ghost" friend had appeared.

A ghost with a laugh like a barking dog.

Down the block tourists laughed and walked through Jackson Park, their very numbers protecting them from the dangers that would lurk there later in the night. The private club called the Bijou let people in and out with amazing regularity. Some Remy recognized, most he didn't. They all seemed happy with their evening.

And no one saw him, as he wanted it to be.

Remy didn't even want his "ghost" to see him.

Remy knew there had been no ghost. Sure, the guy had disappeared right under his fingers, but that trick could be pulled a dozen ways. In his time with the X-Men he had seen a lot stranger things than that.

No, the guy who did his disappearing trick had a reason to do it beyond trying to scare a tourist or two. And Remy figured it was worth a few hours of his time to figure out that reason if he could.

Later, after the city quieted down, he'd pay a visit to Mr. Toole's headquarters. But for the party hours of the evening, he was just going to stand in the shadows and watch and wait for a ghost.

Chapter 6

X-Men?

Professor Xavier's clear call formed in Jean Grey's mind like a voice beamed directly into the center of her mind.

At the moment, she, Scott, and Hank were drifting about a thousand feet above the Juggernaut, sitting comfortably in the *Blackbird*, as the behemoth pounded through the night toward the west. Rogue was about twenty miles ahead of Cain, making sure his path wouldn't take him into a heavily inhabited area.

So far, Juggernaut hadn't actually harmed anyone, and the Professor had told them not to engage him in battle—which was just as well, as even at their best, the Juggernaut had always been a difficult opponent to defeat.

Yes, Professor, Scott said telepathically, speaking for all three of them.

I need the three of you to leave Rogue to watch over the Juggernaut. I'm sending out Storm, Wolverine, and Bishop to help her. I need you three to make a . . . house call.

The location of an estate flashed clearly in Jean's mind, along with the name Gary Service. She was surprised to see it was about twenty miles from where Cain had turned around so suddenly earlier in the day.

That's correct. The Professor's thoughts formed in her head as if he were sitting next to her talking. *I think it was Cain's destination. A man by the name of Gary Service will meet you when you land.*

What's this about?

I would rather he told you, the Professor responded. *I want your reactions to it. Tell him I did not relay his story and he must tell you about his brother.*

Understood.

The Professor relayed the cover story he had devised to protect his own connection to the X-Men, then added, *Report to me as soon as you are finished.*

Then the feeling of emptiness in her head indicated the Professor was gone.

Scott said, "All right then, let's get to work."

The weather in Boise, Idaho was one of those almost-imaginary, perfect summer evenings. A slight breeze cooled the air to room temperature, and the stars filled the sky overhead, breaking through even the city lights. The faint smell of warm sage from the nearby desert mixed with the rich aroma of freshly mowed lawns. Hundreds of back-door barbecues sizzled around the small city, sending white puffs of smoke swirling upward into the clear night sky.

The door of Robert Service's private jet let in the wonderful smells and the clean, fresh, mountain air. The jet sat off to one side of the Gowen Field Airport runway. Private jets were common at Gowen Field, due to the number of large corporations headquartered in Boise. So tonight, one more jet attracted no attention at all.

Robert Service had remained inside as the plane was fueled. He figured there was no point in getting the locals talking about his huge size. And besides, getting in and out of the door of the plane was no easy task.

After the plane was fueled, checked, and ready to go, he sent the pilot and copilot on separate missions into the small city.

The pilot was to get them all dinner. For the first time since Robert had touched the gem, he was slightly hungry. He wasn't sure what being hungry, or not being hungry for that matter, meant in his new form, but he figured there was no point in fighting it.

The copilot was on a much more important mission. He was to find detailed maps of the entire area north of their location, including, if he could, up into Canada. And the more detailed the map the better.

Before leaving New York, Robert had wondered how he was going to pinpoint the exact location of the part of the emerald he was looking for. He could sense that the stone was west, but west was a very big place when it came to such a small stone.

But then when he awoke when the plane was over Reno and realized he could feel the stone to the north, his solution was suddenly clear.

They would simply fly an ever tightening circle, using the feeling in his head for the direction of the gem, to close in on the location. First they would fly north from Boise, heading toward Spokane, going until it felt as if the gem was south. He'd draw a line on the map at that point, then have the plane turn west until it felt as if the gem was again behind him again.

Another line, then back south until the gem felt north. And so on, always tightening in on the location. It might take them some time, but it would work. He knew that without a doubt.

One hour later, map on his lap as his huge bulk filled the couch in the private plane, Robert Service's jet lifted off into the perfect Idaho summer night and turned north.

One hundred and sixty miles later, Robert knew the gem was now behind them.

He drew his first line on his map and laughed.

Rogue stood, hands on hips, facing the newly arriving X-Men. Around her the rolling hills of Pennsylvania were dotted with the lights of farms and homes. Under her feet, the freshly plowed earth of the open field filled the air with the thick smell of dirt. To the south of her the sky was bright with the lights of Scranton. Otherwise the night was so dark that over her head the stars formed a blanket of white, as if the sky had been dusted with powered sugar. A beautiful evening and one that she had been enjoying so far, despite the menace of the Juggernaut.

As Storm, Wolverine, and Bishop approached, her thoughts turned to Remy on his ''personal business'' down in New Orleans. She wished he had let her go with him—or, better still, that he hadn't gone at all. But he had insisted on going alone. Remy was such a loner, especially when it came to anything to do with his hometown, that it annoyed her at times. But still, if they got this problem with ol' Juggy settled, she just might head down south to see if he needed a hand. It would be easier than worrying about him so much.

Rogue forced her mind off of Remy and back on the

approaching X-Men. Ororo Munroe—called Storm because she had the ability to harness the power of nature to do as she bid—was walking slightly ahead of the other two across the open field. Her bright white hair seemed to shine with a light all its own under the stars. Rogue was struck by how much Ororo looked at home on such a beautiful summer evening. It felt to Rogue that Storm, if she truly wanted, might even be able to move the stars around in the sky.

To Storm's right was Bishop, the X-Man from the future. He walked with a military stride, never looking anywhere but straight ahead. To Storm's left, walking more like an animal of the night than a human, was Logan, otherwise known as Wolverine. Logan's muscular body was covered with coarse, dark hair. He was the X-Men's fiercest fighter and loved to mix it up with the Juggernaut. He had unbreakable bones and claws—made out of adamantium—and super-fast healing. He also took no guff from anyone.

Storm nodded to Rogue and then Hank as the five formed a loose circle in open field.

"Status?" Storm asked.

"Scott, Jean an' Hank just took off about five minutes ago in the *Blackbird*. Juggy's about five miles from this position and heading back for Ohio on the same path he used to get here."

"Good," Storm said. "The Professor wants us to continue to keep an eye on him, and make sure he doesn't actually harm anyone. Otherwise, until we discover what's happening, we leave him alone. Just watch him."

"Y'mean *baby-sit*," Logan said, the disgust at their assignment clear in his voice.

"It is not our place to question orders," Bishop said.

Logan glared at the tall, straight-backed X-Men in his blue and yellow suit. "Bub, I question what I want. And right now I say we just stop the big guy right where he is."

Bishop said nothing, only returned the stare.

"We do as the Professor asked," Storm said. "Our mission is to safeguard lives in Juggernaut's path. Far more important, don't you think, than baby-sitting?"

Logan only snorted.

"We make no move to stop the Juggernaut until we have more information," Storm said, glancing at each, then again looking at Logan directly. "Those are the Professor's instructions and we follow them."

"Will do," Rogue said. She had always been impressed how well Storm handled the group. It was no wonder that the Professor had made her team leader when Cyclops left the team for a time, and kept her on as co-leader after he returned.

"Oh, boy," Rogue said, smiling. She offered her right arm to Logan. "A night under the stars with two men. What more can a woman want?"

"Kid," Logan said, moving over beside her, "if you don't know, I sure ain't tellin' ya."

She laughed, and a moment later she lifted him off the ground, turned, and headed west, passing over the Juggernaut a moment later.

On her arm she could feel Logan tighten up. It was clear he so much wanted to just get down and fight him.

If the feeling in her stomach was right, Logan was going to have more than enough fight on his hands before this was all over.

As Scott, Jean, and Hank climbed down out of the *Blackbird* near the edge of the private runway on the Service estate, a figure emerged from the shadows and moved toward them. Scott glanced over at Jean. "That's him. You getting anything in particular from him?" His voice was low enough that the approaching figure couldn't hear.

Jean shrugged. "I can feel a level of nervousness, but no threat."

Scott nodded and studied the approaching man. He seemed to be in his early thirties, with brown hair and a sloped-shoulder walk. He looked to be about five-nine, and most likely hadn't worked out a day in his life. Scott figured he would look more at home with large, thick glasses and a pocket protector full of pens. But he wore an expensive sports coat and high-priced tennis shoes.

As he neared, he smiled. "I'm Gary Service."

Scott noted his voice sounded nervous as Jean had said.

Hank took the lead. "I'm the Beast, but my friends call me Hank. These are two of my associates, Cyclops and Phoenix."

Gary Service reached out and shook all three of their hands. "Nice meeting you."

His handshake, Scott noticed, was adequate, but not very firm. the man's gaze darted back and forth among them.

"What did Dr. Xavier tell you?" Service asked.

"Nothing," Hank said, "except that we were to ask you about your brother."

Service nodded. "Let's go to my office. I've warned my father that he would have visitors, but I want to tell you what I saw before I subject you to a talk with him."

Scott gave Jean a puzzled look, then said, "As you wish."

Without another word, Service turned and led the three X-Men down a concrete path through an ornately decorated garden. Lights, like small mushrooms sprouting in the plants, kept both the path and the garden illuminated like a pathway at Disneyland. Scott found it both attractive, and odd for a New York estate.

The mansion was a large, white, three-story building that dominated the area in the middle of manicured lawns, also illuminated by little mushroom lights. Service led them in a back door, through a big kitchen filled with copper pots and pans, then down a hall and into a large office.

He closed the door behind them and moved around behind a cluttered desk, indicating three leather chairs in front of the desk for them to sit.

Scott studied the room, filled with books and magazines. Mostly financial, a few science. A large computer dominated one corner of the big desk and there was no doubt to Scott that the computer was hooked up world-wide and got a lot of use.

"Again," Service said as he dropped down into his chair with a sigh, "thanks for coming."

"It wasn't a problem," Hank said gently, "but it would be nice to know why we're here."

"I suppose," Gary said, "that starting from the beginning would be the best. You see, during the Korean war, my father found a large emerald in the ruins of a temple."

Scott felt as if someone had run an electrical shock through the seat of his chair. And with the intimate connection with Jean, he could feel she was just as surprised as he was. That sounded exactly like how the Juggernaut had gotten his powers.

Service looked first at Scott, then at Jean, then Hank, a puzzled expression on his face. He could clearly tell they were shocked. "Does that mean anything?"

"It might," Hank said. "But please go on with the story."

Service nodded. "My father was warned by a monk to never touch a gem he found in that temple, so when he discovered the emerald, he says he didn't touch it."

"And he kept it all these years?" Jean asked.

Service nodded. "Up until the other night my brother, Robert, and I didn't even know it existed. But you see, my father is dying of cancer, so he decided to show us, and warn us to not touch it."

"And your brother ignored the warning?" Scott said. His stomach was twisting like he was about to go into a life and death battle. Could it be possible that there were now two Juggernauts? That thought was just too ugly to comprehend.

"That's correct," Service said. "Robert has a real ego problem. His goal in life is to be the richest and most powerful man alive. And, I'm afraid, he will stop at nothing to get it.''

"So what happened when he touched the gem?" Jean asked.

Service shuddered. "It was amazing. Some sort of energy flowed out of the emerald and surrounded him, expanding him, making him bigger and much, much stronger. I'll bet he's almost eight feet tall now."

"Another Juggernaut," Scott said softly.

"Possibly." Hank said. He stared intently at Service across the desk. "How tall would you say he is now?"

Service frowned. "He barely hit six feet before, and he grew at least half a foot."

Hank nodded. "Then he's not quite at Cain's level. The Juggernaut is closer to seven feet tall. Did the gem in some fashion attach itself to him?"

"No," Service said. "He still held it in his hand when he left the room."

Scott was starting to see where Hank was going with the questions. The pattern of what happened to Robert Service when he touched the emerald was similar to what happened to Cain Marko when he touched the Cyttorak ruby. But it wasn't *exactly* the same. And that was a good sign.

"So where is your brother now?" Scott asked.

"He's on our private jet. I just got a report that he's just taken off from Boise, heading north toward Spokane."

"Idaho?" Jean said. "What's he doing out west?"

"I have no idea," Service said, sighing.

Jean stared at Service for a moment, then said, "I

think we should talk to your father now, if that would be all right?''

Service shrugged and stood. ''He's got a special, round-the-clock care unit set up near the front of the house. I hope you can stand the smell.''

''Smell?'' Scott asked.

Service nodded, leading them toward the office door. ''That's right. You see, my father is dying of a nasty form of skin cancer. It is not pleasant.''

CHAPTER 7

CHAPTER 7

After four hours of standing totally still in a small alcove just down the street from the entrance to the Bijou, Remy's "ghost" from the previous night hadn't shown up.

Around the French Quarter, the tourists were now mostly bunched around the shops, bars, and clubs along the narrow Bourbon Street. Only a few braved on foot the darker side streets between Bourbon and the Café Dumond down near the river.

All the good restaurants in the Quarter were long closed, and the thick smells of gumbo and Cajun cooking had been replaced with the faint odor of rotting garbage and spilled rum drifting on the warm humid air.

When Remy had left the alcove, he half expected the "ghost" to show up and follow him, but on that guess he was also out of luck. At some point he was going to figure out what that "ghost" thing had been all about. But it didn't look as if it would be tonight.

Remy moved past the laughing tourists sitting in the outdoor Café Dumond and down along the river levy, heading for Toole's headquarters. It was time someone talked to Toole about the old ways of the city.

Remy figured he was just the person to do it.

And tonight was as good a time as any.

The black water of the river lapped at the rocks along the dike as Remy slipped from shadow to shadow, moving up into the neighborhood of the warehouse that had been converted by the mysterious Mr. Toole. The area was a rundown section of town. At one time, in the distant past, the district had been a busy area for shipping and business, but no one had yet taken the old, gray warehouses and converted them into shops for the tourists. So the buildings rotted in the heat and humidity and rain, occupied mainly by the homeless, the streets around them prime markets for illegal drugs of every type.

That applied to most of the buildings and most of the streets in the district, but not all of them. One warehouse complex had been saved by Toole.

Remy's first sign of a guard was half a block away from Toole's building. Two men walked along the street, almost as if they were tourists, very lost, walking slowly in one of the most dangerous areas of town.

Not hardly.

They both wore trenchcoats, even though the night was warm and humid. Remy knew for a fact that machine guns were hung in slings under those coats, armed and ready to be swung up at a moment's notice.

Remy held his hand on two playing cards in the pocket of his duster, ready to charge them with energy at any moment as he moved silently across the street. He ducked into a small alcove and waited for the two guards to pass.

Then, moving from shadow to alcove, then back to shadow, he made his way closer to Toole's buildings. The two guards would have been easy to take out, but why announce his presence just yet? Better to get inside before doing that.

A quarter of a block from Toole's buildings, the guards got even thicker. Two by two, they walked the streets around the old warehouse. More guards were posted in windows of buildings nearby, machine gun barrels sticking out of the windows like popsicle sticks out of children's mouths.

Remy stopped and studied what lay ahead. He could count at least fifty armed men just around the front. No doubt at all that there were many more inside, and maybe even a few he hadn't spotted.

The army's here, he thought. *This guy is one scared sucker.*

Remy moved back down the street and circled around a few blocks until he was down on the dike that held the river out of most of New Orleans. One thing a thief learned real early in life was that if you couldn't get in the front door, more than likely the back door was wide open.

Remy moved up and over the dike, then climbed down the rocks into the lukewarm water. It smelled slightly like dead fish and motor oil, but nothing as bad as the thick swamp water of Cajun country where Remy had grown up. And this river supposedly didn't have any alligators in it.

He let the gentle current drift him down along the levy until he was even with the back of Toole's building complex. There had once been a dock there, but it was long rotted away to a few timbers sticking out of the water.

Using one of the old dock timbers for cover, he slowly climbed out of the water, stopping for a few minutes to let most of the water finish dripping off his waterproof costume and duster. Then he headed up the side of the dike toward a power pole located thirty yards from the back of the warehouse.

There, using the power pole for cover, he studied the back of Toole's building.

A half-dozen guards were stationed at various locations along the warehouse side of the dike and Remy could see another dozen in positions along the tops of the warehouses. In all his years he had never seen a location with so many armed guards. It was as if all the gold of Fort Knox was inside there.

What was this Toole so afraid of? This level of protection made no sense at all.

Of course, the number of men made no difference at all to Remy. They just made getting in a little more of a challenge, that was all. And getting to Toole would, more than likely, take a little more time. But at this point Remy was in no hurry.

None at all.

He studied the guard positions, the power lines running into the building, the locations of the windows and the back doors, the large, old loading dock that covered a third of one side of the building. Spotlights flooded the area around the building and along the land side of the dike. The area under those spotlights would be a killing field. So the trick was first to shut them down.

He moved slowly and silently back down the rock-covered dike toward the water and the shelter of old dock timbers. Along the way he picked up baseball-sized stones, dropping a few into the pockets of his duster, holding the others in the crook of his arm.

At the timber he stopped, gathered up a few more

stones, then smiled to himself. "*Mon ami*," he said softly to Toole inside the building, "here I come, ready or not."

Using his mutant power, he charged one of the rocks in his fist with a full charge of kinetic energy, then, with the accuracy of a professional baseball player, he threw it at the base of the power pole.

Direct hit.

The explosion shook the night and echoed over the black water, shaking the drinks in the bars on Bourbon Street.

The lower half of the power pole evaporated into splinters, dropping the top half down, pulling the wires tight.

There was a loud snapping and popping, then the lights of the warehouse flickered and went out. Remy had no doubt that the place would have backup power systems, but this would give him a good start.

Moving to the right along the waterline, Remy charged one rock after another, stopping to throw each one back up over the dike toward the left corner of the warehouse complex.

Each rock hit and exploded like a huge bomb, sending bits of rock, concrete, and wood flying into the air in a concussion of orange light.

A few of the guards started firing, and others picked up the pace. What they were firing at Remy had no idea, since he was nowhere near the area. But the entire warehouse district of New Orleans now sounded like a war zone.

He picked up a few smaller rocks that he felt he could throw farther, charged them, and tossed them even harder at the left side of Toole's building. Then right behind them he tossed a few larger ones.

Explosion mixed with explosion.

The roar of gunfire became like an explosion in and of itself.

Remy moved down the dike, away from the fight, toward the right side of the warehouse where an old loading dock used to let trucks in from a small side alley.

He was going in there, while everyone else focused on the other side of the complex.

He neared the top of the dike and stopped just long enough to pick up three more rocks. One right after another he charged them and tossed them as far as he could toward different parts of the left side of the building.

After the three blinding flashes and explosions intensified the gunfire and blinded anyone looking in that direction, he went over the top of the dike and down across the darkened open area to the loading dock, moving in under it like a shadow of the night, unseen by the hundreds of guards.

The river tumbled down over the rocks, filling the steep-walled valley with a low rumbling sound. On most evenings over the many years that Albert Jonathan had lived in this secluded mountain valley, the sounds of the river had comforted him, soothed him to sleep.

But not tonight.

Tonight there would be no sleep for him. Tonight the river sounded like a wounded mountain lion, roaring its warning to anyone who would listen.

Every shadow around the log cabin now held danger. Every rock seemed to shift, as if forming into creatures that would tear him apart.

And during it all, the echoing laughter inside his head.

Albert sat on the front porch of his log cabin, his Springfield rifle across his lap, extra shells in his pocket, waiting. Someone or something was coming for him, and for his emerald. He knew that without a doubt.

And he was going to fight to the last, he also knew that without a doubt.

Far over the valley, the slight rumble of a passing jet temporarily overshadowed the sounds of the tumbling river. Albert glanced up at the star-filled sky and the blinking light of the jet. For a fleeting moment he thought about running, staying ahead of what was coming after him.

Then the thought passed, as did the jet.

The sounds of the river again dominated his beautiful valley. There would be no running for Albert Jonathan. He had moved into this valley before anyone living had been born. He wouldn't leave it now. At least not without a fight.

And if he did leave, it would be most likely in a pine box. And that was just fine with him, too.

After leaving the Service estate, Scott had turned the *Blackbird* south to the Xavier Institute. All three desperately felt the need for a shower. Gary Service had warned them about the smell of his father, but none of them, accustomed to fighting and death in all forms, had been prepared for a living man simply rotting away.

To their credit, they had managed to remain in the room with Robert Service Sr. while he told the story of finding the emerald, and what the monk had told him. There was really nothing new he added beyond what his son had already told them.

They had thanked Gary Service and his father and immediately left, heading back for the mansion, a brief trip given the short distance and the *Blackbird*'s supersonic engines.

Professor Xavier was waiting for them in his office.

"What did you discover?" he asked.

"A number of things," Scott said. "First, there seems to be a second gem, an emerald, resembling the crimson ruby of Cyttorak that Cain touched."

The Professor said nothing, so Jean continued.

"Robert Service Jr. was the first to touch the gem after its discovery thirty years ago by his father," Jean said.

"And by touching the gem," Hank said, "the younger Service was changed in a fashion similar to how Cain was changed."

"But there are differences?" the Professor said, phrasing the statement like a question.

"Clear ones," Hank said. "Robert is not as large as Cain yet. He's about a half-foot shorter, and the gem did not attach itself to him."

The Professor raised one eyebrow at that.

"What puzzles me," Jean said, "is why would someone who had just gone through such a transformation immediately jump on a plane and head to Idaho?"

"A very good question," the Professor said. "One I have been asking also."

"And did Cain know where Robert Service and the emerald was?" Scott said. "From his path and sudden turn around, it would seem that somehow Cain was, and is, after that emerald also."

"Cain has never shown the slightest hint of telepathic powers," the Professor said. "If he does feel the new gem for some reason or another, it is through the stones themselves, and the power bands of Cyttorak."

"Triggered when Robert Service picked up the stone for the first time?" Jean said.

"Considering the timing," the Professor said, "that would be the most logical conclusion."

"So what do we do now?" Scott asked. "Clear a path for Cain all the way to Idaho?"

"No," the Professor said. "Offer him a ride."

"What?" Scott said.

Beside him, Hank laughed and said, "Of course."

Wingate Toole watched on a half-dozen monitors the explosions and fight going on outside his headquarters. Kyle, his thin frame leaning against a chair, stood beside him, saying nothing.

Another explosion rocked the building and jiggled the glassware on the bar.

The monitors and most of the electronic security system of the building was being run on backup power. There was enough to keep the security up, as well as all the computers and office areas, but not enough to light the outside of the building. And whoever attacked must somehow have known that. Or gotten very lucky.

Was this the attack Toole had been worried about? It didn't feel right. The person or thing he felt inside his head that was coming after him, was distant. Even more distant than the first time he'd had the feeling the night before.

Now, outside, it looked like there was a full assault going on against his headquarters. Yet he could pick up no intruders on the monitors. Just his own men firing into the dark night, hitting who knew what.

In the distance, police sirens were wailing as a dozen cop cars headed in this direction.

Then suddenly it dawned on Toole what was going on and his stomach clamped up tight in fear.

Toole spun around and faced Kyle. "Tell those idiots to stop firing and retreat into the building before the cops get here. This was only a diversion."

Kyle nodded. Quickly he headed for the door.

Toole turned back to face the security monitors. Then he had another thought. "Kyle, make sure if we have wounded or dead, to get them inside. We don't want to give the cops any reason to come inside. Understand?"

"Yes, sir," Kyle said as he ducked out the door.

Ten seconds later all the firing stopped. Toole could see dozens of men crawling up from cover and heading for the entrances to the building. A few of them carried wounded men.

"Idiots," Toole said to the monitors.

Two blocks away, the first cop car came to a stop,

blocking the street. Another slid into place beside it.

By the time all his men were inside and the doors locked down, Toole could see on the monitors that all the streets leading out of the area were blocked.

"Going to be a long night," he said aloud, laughing at the cops. "Because you're not going to find anything on those streets at all."

Behind him, Kyle entered and moved up behind Toole to watch the security monitors.

"Everyone inside and accounted for?" Toole asked.

"Doing a head count now," Kyle said.

Toole nodded, then had another thought that almost froze him in his chair. Slowly he turned and faced his second in command. "Go back down there and make sure we don't have an extra guard or two. There was a reason for that diversion and that might just have been it."

Kyle nodded. Without a word he spun and headed back outside.

Behind him Toole automatically locked the doors, then turned back to the security monitors.

Remy paused in the dark under the old loading dock, then continued in farther under the dock toward the building. Every so often a cobweb covered his face, but he ignored them, feeling his way forward in the almost total darkness over the rough, damp ground.

The smell of mold filled his mouth and nose. He could hear the faint scurrying of rats even over the gunfire going on outside. He had no real idea where this area under the dock would lead, but most likely he'd find a rotted floorboard on this old dock he could come up through somewhere near the building.

And from there it would be easy to get inside.

He reached the wall of the building where the old wooden loading dock was attached. There he got luckier than he had even hoped.

A broken and boarded-over narrow service entrance. This warehouse obviously had something other than concrete floors inside. He knew it wasn't a basement, because they didn't have basements in New Orleans. Most of the town was below sea level, and early on the French discovered they couldn't even put coffins in the ground. They simply floated back to the surface.

But this warehouse had an area under part of the interior flooring, more than likely to run heat and electrical ducts. And that would be perfect for Remy.

As the gunfire suddenly stopped, he pulled off one old, rotted board and leaned it gently against the wall under the opening. A moment later he had the other off and the opening clear.

He went through feetfirst, then pulled the wood with him back up, lodging it into place as best he could so that a quick inspection would show no one had been through there.

The darkness was now total.

He slowly pulled out a playing card and held it up, charging it with just enough kinetic energy so it glowed slightly.

He had guessed correctly. He was in a maintenance and flood drainage tunnel, long forgotten. He walked a hundred feet along the tunnel, noting the places where access chutes lead upward into the building.

Then he laughed to himself softly. No point in going on at this time. Toole would have his men on full alert, knowing the explosions were nothing more than a diversion. So the best plan for this thief would be to sit down and wait until morning, when all the guards were tired, and the heat had been turned down a notch or two. Then he'd give Toole a surprise the man wouldn't soon forget.

And maybe Remy would even give him a lesson in respect for the old ways of doing things.

Remy looked around for a dry spot, then sat down with his back against a concrete wall.

Ten minutes later he was asleep.

CHAPTER 8

Cyclops brought the *Blackbird* into a soft landing in a freshly plowed field north of Williamsport, Pennsylvania, sending swirling clouds of dust up into the black night air.

Standing in the open field, waiting for him, the Beast, and Phoenix, were the other X-Men on the Juggernaut watch: Storm, Rogue, Wolverine, and Bishop. Behind them was a small, black jet transport, a sleek plane that had been given to them by the Shi'ar at the same time the Shi'ar had upgraded the X-Men's Danger Room. It had a swept-back hawkish look and at night it seemed almost invisible against the dark sky.

The small transport could hold only four X-Men comfortably but, like the *Blackbird*, it had jet speed combined with vertical lift-off and landing capabilities. The only problem was that they still couldn't decide on a name for it. The argument had been going on for weeks, with Scott's favorite being *Raven*, which nicely complemented *Blackbird*.

No one else much agreed with him, but he still called it the *Raven* anyway. Maybe if he repeated it enough, the name would just catch on.

"Well," Logan said as they walked over the loose dirt toward their team members. "Are we finally done babysittin'?"

"In a manner of speaking," Scott said, smiling at Logan. Wolverine had an attitude most of the time, and had been having some problems keeping his animal side

127

in check lately, but he was as good as they came. Scott had fought many a battle beside Logan, and there wasn't an X-Man he'd rather have beside him in a fight.

"Great," Logan said. "Let's teach that big lunk once-an-fer-all to not go stompin' around."

"Well, not exactly," Scott said. "Sorry, Wolverine."

Logan snorted. "Figures there'd be a catch."

"And what exactly," Storm said, "does the Professor want us to undertake now?"

"We're going to offer Cain a ride," Scott said.

Before the others could protest, Storm said, "Perhaps, Cyclops, you should fill us all in on the thinking behind this action."

Scott nodded. "A fairly short story, so everyone just hold on."

It took him less than five minutes to explain what he, Jean, Hank, and the Professor had learned on the Service estate.

"Two Juggernauts, huh?" Logan said. "Keeps things interestin'."

"So offering Cain a ride would serve two purposes," Storm said.

"Correct," Scott said. "It would stop the destruction of the countryside and—"

"Lead us to Robert Service and the emerald," Ororo said.

Rogue only shook her head and smiled, while Bishop, as would any good soldier, said nothing.

Scott loved how this group of wildly different mutants worked together. They bickered, they fought over small details and methods of attack, but when it came right down to it, they stood side by side. To Scott, they were his family.

Ororo faced Scott. "What plan did you have in mind?"

Scott glanced over at Jean, then faced Ororo again. "Cain will fit in the *Blackbird*."

"With a shoehorn and a couple good kicks," Logan said. "An' I'll be glad to do the kickin'."

Scott ignored him and went on. "Phoenix and I will offer him a ride, while you, Wolverine, Beast, and Bishop take the *Raven* and follow at a distance. Rogue will fly advance scout to see if she can pinpoint Service's location."

"Do we have a general idea where we are heading?" Ororo said. "Or must we depend completely on the Juggernaut?"

"At last report," Jean said, "Robert Service's jet was flying in circles over the wilderness area in central Idaho."

"Circles?" Ororo asked.

Scott only shrugged. He had no idea why a man who had just touched a gem similar to Cain's ruby, would suddenly jump on a plane, fly to Idaho, and circle over the mountains.

"Looks as if we have a few hours of flying ahead of us," Hank said. "Plenty of time for a little nap."

"That there will be," Scott said.

"Assuming you can talk Cain into the ride," Ororo said.

Scott nodded and glanced at Jean. "Yeah, assuming."

Jean touched his arm and between them silent reassurance flowed.

The map on Robert Service's lap had more than a half dozen lines on it, forming a very clear, fairly small box in the middle of one of the wildest, most mountainous areas of central Idaho.

Under the clear night sky, Robert could see the shapes of snow-capped mountaintops below. He had been born and raised in New York and had been to the Appalachians. And, of course, he'd seen pictures of Mount Everest and similar peaks. But he had no idea that there were such mountains as these in the United States. These made the mountains in the east look like small bumps.

And the area they covered shocked him. He had trouble imagining the immense size of it. A far, far bigger area than the entire state of New York. The jet seemed to fly forever, crossing over one range after another. How could people live out here? On the map it showed only one small, two-lane road winding along rivers between Boise in the south and the entire northern part of the state. Not even a freeway. Nothing but impossibly large mountains. The whole region was far too primitive for his tastes.

Service stared out the window as the jet made one more pass over the area. The feeling of the other gem suddenly switched in his mind and he hit the intercom button. "Exact location, please."

A moment later the pilot relayed their location and

Service drew another line on his map. This one was right over another line he'd drawn earlier. The jet had gotten him as close as it was going to get him.

He glanced out the window again. In a way, having the gem be in such an isolated area was going to make finding it much easier.

Now, after two hours, the best he could narrow the location of the gem down to while in the jet was a nine-hundred-square-mile area of mountains. Somewhere in there was a stone the size of his fist. He'd find it, but to do so he was going to need help.

He punched the intercom button to the pilot. "Return to Boise," he said.

"Yes, sir," the pilot said and with an easy banking motion the plane turned south.

Robert Service stared at the map and the seemingly small square he'd marked off. Tomorrow morning, in Boise, he'd see if he could narrow that down. There couldn't be that many people living in that rugged country, could there?

He leaned back and closed his eyes.

The next thing he knew, the wheels of the jet were screeching on the runway in Boise.

Jean took a deep breath of the warm night air and let it out. She and Scott had flown in the *Blackbird* to a position a mile or so ahead of Cain. They now stood near his path. She could feel the ground under her feet rumbling slightly with the pounding of his steps.

"Scott," she said, "let me do the talking on this one."

Scott glanced over at her, then nodded. Between them the understanding was there. He knew she had a way with convincing people to do things her way—she just seemed to know people. Since the Juggernaut's helmet protected him from any mind control, she was going to have to use only her persuasive abilities.

She glanced up and to the east, looking at the black sky for any sign of the other X-Men. Nothing visible to the naked eye, yet she knew they were there, ready to be beside her and Scott in a flash, just in case anything went wrong.

She blanked her mind for a moment and focused on the dark study of the Professor's in the mansion. Then she thought, *Professor, we're about to talk to Cain. Any suggestions?*

The Professor's thought formed clearly in her mind. *Cain was willing to aid us against Magneto when he took over Manhattan. Perhaps we can use that to our advantage. Good luck.*

Thanks.

"Here he comes," Scott said, pointing across the dark field at the looming shape.

She turned her attention to the task at hand as the rumbling thumps of the Juggernaut's heavy steps vibrated the ground around them.

She wrapped them both in a telekinetic bubble and lifted them off the ground, slowly drifting to match Cain's pace at a height where they could look him in the eye.

Cain didn't bother to even glance at them, just kept

his gaze straight ahead, his pace consistent. The look on his face wasn't a happy one, that much Jean could tell.

"Cain?" Jean said. "We need to talk."

"Go right ahead," Cain said. "Seems you X-Men do a lot of that. Doesn't mean I gotta listen to it."

"We know where you're headed."

Cain grunted and didn't even look at them. "Nice, but *wrong*. I don't even know where I'm headed."

Jean glanced at Scott, who looked just as puzzled as she felt. Could Cain be telling the truth? Did he really *not* know where he was heading?

"Well," Jean said, continuing on the path she'd started. "We do. You're heading for Idaho."

Cain laughed this time. "And let me see if I get this right. On this route I'll also get to see South Dakota, Wyoming, and eventually even Oregon. Right? That's all I need is a bunch of mutie travel guides. Would you two just leave me alone? I won't ask twice."

"We will, Cain," Jean said, "If you just let me tell you about Robert Service and the emerald he found in a stone temple in Korea."

"Emerald?" Cain asked, for the first time turning his head and looking at the two X-Men, though he continued walking.

"Robert Service Sr. found the emerald in an old stone temple, but never touched it. Last night he showed it to his son, Robert Service Jr., and the son touched it and was changed."

Cain shook his head side to side. "Nice try. You expect me to believe there's another fella like me?"

"He's not exactly like you," Jean said, again glancing at Scott who nodded that she should continue. "Service didn't grow as large or powerful as you are, and the stone didn't attach to him. All this happened about thirty miles from where you turned around this afternoon."

"Okay, so why did I turn around if I was headed there?" Cain's voice still held its biting, sarcastic tone, but Jean could tell there was a hint of interest under the surface.

"Because," Jean said, "Robert Service Jr. got on a plane at that moment and headed toward Idaho."

The Juggernaut stopped so quickly that it took Jean a moment to slow her and Scott down and bring them back around to face Cain.

"At exactly that moment?" Cain asked, staring at them both. "Yer kiddin', right?"

"No," Scott said.

"We didn't know that for certain until later, after we talked to Gary Service, Robert's younger brother," Jean said. "We then checked the flight plan the pilot filed and the times are exact."

Cain nodded, then stared at the X-Men. "So I'm after a guy by the name of Service, huh?" Cain said. "Good to know who I'm going to pound when I find him. Thanks."

He suddenly started forward again and Jean quickly moved herself and Scott out of his way, going back to matching his pace.

"Cain," Jean said, "at this rate, it's going to take you four days to reach Idaho."

"So," Cain said, not looking at them. "Bein' my travel agent again."

THE JEWELS OF CYTTORAK

"Service is in a private jet," Jean said. "More than likely he won't be there by then."

"So I follow him to where he goes next. So what? He can't get away from me."

"Not saying he can," Jean said, trying to keep her frustration with talking to Cain down under the tone of her voice. "We're just offering you a ride is all."

Again Cain glanced over at the two X-Men floating along beside him. Jean could almost feel his intense stare boring through her. She wished, just for a moment, that he would take off that helmet so she could tell what he was thinking.

Suddenly he stopped again.

And again Jean had to swing herself and Scott out and around to face him.

"Took me a minute," Cain said, "but now I understand. You're offering me a ride to get me to stop tearin' up the countryside. Right?"

"Exactly," Jean said, smiling at him.

Inside her head she heard Scott think, *He's smarter than he looks.* But luckily he didn't say it out loud.

Cain shook his head and laughed again, the sound like thunder rolling over the surrounding farms. "You do-gooders amaze me. Always stickin' your nose into other people's business, even when you ain't asked."

"So, Cain," Jean said, "you want a lift to Idaho?"

"Work together again? That'll be twice in a row, y'know."

"It worked against Magneto and the Acolytes," Jean said. "The three of us and Rogue worked pretty well together then."

Cain actually smiled at that. "You got a point. Yeah, okay, why not? 'Sides, it's no fun tearin' up real estate unless I'm poundin' on someone when I do it."

"The *Blackbird*'s over that way," Jean said, pointing across the field.

"One thing," Cain said. "Promise me you won't get between me and Service when I find him."

CHAPTER 9

R emy awoke as the first signs of morning light filtered in through the cracks in the boards under the loading dock. Around him, the maintenance tunnel smelled of dampness and mold. He stood, quietly brushed off his duster, and stretched. Over the years he hadn't needed much sleep each night, but when he did sleep, he could do it anywhere. Even standing up. It was part of the training of a thief. Patience and making the best of a situation.

Now it was time to see what situation faced him with Mr. Toole.

The maintenance tunnel was no more than ten feet across and filled in places with large heating ducts and bundles of wires. There was no doubt that the tunnel ran under the entire warehouse and was the utility spine of the place.

Every twenty feet or so, a shaft led upward. Most of them didn't run farther than one floor up, stopping at the roofline most likely. But in two places the shafts went up farther, to what was clearly a second floor over part of the warehouse. If Toole was going to have an office in this place, it would be up there.

Silently, Remy climbed up the rusted steel ladder inside one of the shafts, moving slowly upward until he was level with the second floor.

In three places small tunnels led off, more than likely under the floor of the office areas. There was no way Remy wanted to be under that floor, trapped like a rat in those tight tunnels. Not his style at all.

He kept climbing until he reached the top of the ladder. There the shaft opened into an open attic area. Much better. Exposed ceiling joists and insulation covered the bottom of the attic, with boards laid out across the joists as walkways.

Remy stopped, holding onto the ladder, and studied the open area. Now the question was, which direction was Toole's office? If the man was as power hungry and egotistical as Remy suspected he was, he would have a lavish office, most likely with a view of the river.

So toward the river it was.

Remy eased his frame silently up onto one of the thin boards and moved slowly forward, being very careful to keep his weight over the ceiling joists so he would make no sounds at all. Twenty feet along, there was a large light fixture cut into the ceiling of the room below, obviously done in just the last few years. Lots of light came up through it and the faint sounds of voices could be heard from below.

Remy eased down onto his stomach on the walkway and crawled forward until he could see down through a slot in the fixture. He could see the top of an ornate desk, a computer screen, and a dozen security monitors on one wall. One man with a balding head sat behind the desk, while another thin man stood facing him. Remy couldn't quite make out what they were saying, but Remy had no doubt that the man sitting at the desk was Toole.

Suddenly the door opened to the office and two new figures entered.

Instantly Remy's stomach clamped up like he'd just been hit solidly in the gut. One of the figures wore the ritual attire of an assassin, along with the plain brown cloth over the face with the diamond over one eye. In his hand he carried a longsword.

How many times over the years had Remy fought against those swords and the assassins who carried them? More times than he cared to remember.

The Assassins Guild was the sworn enemy of the Thieves Guild. Both had coexisted for decades without too much trouble, holding an uneasy truce most of the time.

But what was an assassin doing in Toole's office? From everything Remy had heard, Toole had ignored everything about the old way of doing things, including the assassins, the thieves, and the mob.

Suddenly into Remy's view another figure stepped, facing Toole's desk.

This time Remy had to force the air into his lungs just to keep from gasping.

It was a woman. She wore a black bodysuit, with purple arm-and-leg light armor. Attached to the armor was a long cape that flowed over her powerful shoulders and down around her back.

But it wasn't the outfit that shocked Remy.

It was the hair. Golden blonde hair worn tied back. He would have known that hair anywhere.

Bella Donna.

His wife.

The leader of the assassins.

The woman who had recently sworn to kill him.

• • •

The sun was just breaking over the high mountains east of Boise at six in the morning, cutting through the chill that covered the valley and airport. Unlike weather in New York, the nights in Idaho, even on hot summer days, turned cool. Dew covered the ground where, in a few hours, the sun would be baking the pavement hot as an oven top.

Robert Service strolled across the damp runway and into the open hangar of Back Country Helicopters, glancing around at the repairs being done on one 'copter. Two more sat outside and it was one of those he was interested in.

A half hour ago he had woken up in the back of his private plane. As with the first time he'd fallen asleep, he could no longer sense the other two parts of his emerald. So he pulled out the glowing stone and touched it again, letting its energy flow through and revive him.

This morning, instead of the feeling of the other two gems coming back into his head, red flooded through his mind like a spilled beaker of blood.

Red.

And danger.

Whatever it was that he'd sensed the first night, the red creature was now close. Very close.

And getting closer.

He had put the emerald back into his bag, checked to make sure his gun was in his duffel also, loaded and ready, then climbed out of the jet. He woke and ordered his pilots to fly first to Portland, Oregon, refuel, then return to a small central Idaho town called McCall. He'd meet them there in approximately four hours.

THE JEWELS OF CYTTORAK

It was a longshot. The likelihood was much greater that the red creature, whatever it was, was following the gem, not the plane. But the diversion couldn't hurt, in case it was the plane that it tracked.

And Robert needed some time to locate an emerald in over nine hundred square miles of Idaho wilderness. Four hours should do it, if he was lucky and his plan worked.

Robert shifted the light weight of the duffel, letting the feeling of the gem and the gun comfort him some.

"Hello," he shouted into the empty hangar and his voice echoed off the high metal roof.

"Hello yourself," a man said, moving out from behind the cabin of the helicopter inside the hangar. He was an older man, probably in his late fifties, with a thinning head of gray hair and a large smile. He strolled toward Service, wiping his grease-stained hands on a blue rag as he came.

"Can't say I've ever had anyone in here as big as you," he said, smiling and extending his now-clean hand. "Name's Craig. I own this place."

"Robert Service," Robert said, carefully shaking the man's hand in return, making sure he didn't squeeze too hard. "Are you also a pilot?"

Robert had learned to fly helicopters back a few years before, but didn't want to even try taking one into those mountains alone unless he had to—particularly with his hands much larger than they were.

"Sure am," the guy said. "What can I do for you?"

"I'm willing to pay twenty thousand dollars up front in exchange for four hours of helicopter time and a pilot."

"Twenty thousand?" Craig said, the look of surprise clear in his eyes. "You could almost buy one for that price. What do you need it for? Not that I'm saying no, mind you," he added quickly. "Just wondering. Have to make sure it's legal."

"Oh, it's legal all right. An emergency trip into the central mountains, above the small town of Yellow Pine," Robert lied. "Your helicopters have that kind of range?"

Craig shrugged. "No problem at all, even with someone of your size on board. But that's rugged country up there."

"I'm aware of that," Robert said. "I'm looking for a man who's in there. I've got a way of tracking his location, but it's not exact. More directional in nature."

"So we do a little back and forth is all," the old guy said, nodding to himself.

"Exactly," Robert said. "So how long can you stay aloft up in that area before having to return to refuel?"

"Three-plus hours, safely, at that altitude."

Robert nodded and pulled out his wallet. "I need to leave right now. Is that also possible?"

Craig started to say something, then noticed the wad of cash that Robert took out of his money clip. "Mister, for twenty thousand in *cash*, we could have left ten minutes ago. Let me just run this through, wash my hands, cancel another appointment, and I'll be ready. The big bird on the right out there is gassed and ready to go. Give me five minutes."

"Thank you, Craig," Robert said, smiling his best smile at the older man.

In the back of his mind Robert could tell the red creature was closing in from the east, getting closer and closer. But it felt as if five minutes would be soon enough to get ahead of whatever was coming.

He turned and headed for the helicopter. Maybe after getting the next part of the emerald, it wouldn't matter if the red creature caught up with him. Only time would tell.

Cain had crammed his huge frame into the back of the *Blackbird*. He'd broken one arm off one chair in the back as he sat, but otherwise, so far, there had been no serious damage to the plane.

Then, for the next three hours, as the jet sped west, Cain hadn't said a word. He simply sat hunched over, staring into the night ahead.

Jean and Scott had also remained outwardly quiet. But using Jean's telepathic powers they had "talked" and planned most of the trip, running through any possible plan of action they could think of. In the end they came back to the exact point where they started. They had no idea why Robert Service had been flying in circles in Idaho. And they could only guess at the outcome when Cain caught up to him.

The sun was lighting the sky around them as they crossed over the Teton Mountains and into eastern Idaho. They were within two hundred miles of Boise, approaching the Snake River valley when suddenly things changed slightly.

"*Blackbird*." Ororo's voice cut through the silence of the cabin from the radio link.

Scott flipped a switch to turn his headset to the private channel, then with a glance at Jean said, "Go ahead, Storm."

"Cyclops, we just got confirmation from the Boise airport that Service's plane has taken off, headed west. He filed a flight plan for Portland."

"Understood," Scott said.

He flipped the communication system back to airport approach and then glanced around at Cain hunched over behind him.

Cain said nothing, his dark eyes still focused ahead.

Scott shrugged and turned back forward. *Guess we're going on to Portland*, he said to Jean telepathically through the rapport that husband and wife shared.

Guess we are, Jean replied.

One thing's for certain, we're getting to see some country we'd normally never see.

Almost feels like a vacation, Jean said with a telepathic laugh.

Almost, Scott said. *Almost*.

Wingate Toole stood behind his desk and watched as two of the deadliest humans alive walked into his office.

Kyle, who had been holding the door for them, stepped back, and his already pale face drained even more.

Toole nodded to the man who had a cloth mask over his face and a painted diamond over one eye-slit. He wore the traditional garb of the Assassins Guild and carried a large, gleaming sword that looked sharp enough to cut through steel.

Beside him strode one of the most beautiful and striking women Toole had ever seen. She stood at least six foot tall and wore a black bodysuit with blue armor-like scales on her arms and legs. The scales moved with her rippling muscles like a second skin and the effect was very attractive. A long cape was attached at her shoulders and flowed down behind her as she walked. Her blonde hair was pulled back and cascaded out over the cape.

Her name was Bella Donna and she was the head of the Assassins Guild.

Toole also had no doubt at all that at a moment's whim, she could kill him without a struggle.

He also knew she wouldn't. At least not yet. After she had heard what he had to say, he hoped she would never kill him. Only work with him.

And protect him from what was coming.

Toole indicated that Bella take the seat in front of his desk, but she shook her head and remained standing. The other assassin took a position to her right and slightly behind her where he could keep any eye on both Toole and Kyle.

Toole shrugged and dropped down into his chair, leaning back to look at her. "Thank you for accepting my invitation," Toole said, putting on his best smile.

"The messenger said you have a business proposition," she said. "I will listen."

Toole nodded. "Fair enough," he said. It was the most he had hoped for.

"As I know you are aware," Toole said, "over the

past few years I've slowly taken over more and more of, shall we say, the *business* of our fine city.''

Bella said nothing, only stared at him, her dark brown eyes boring into him like drills.

"The old days of a balance between the mob and the two guilds are almost finished. If I can move in, as I have done, someone else would shortly do the same if I am eliminated."

Bella again said nothing, made no motion. She only stared at him, obviously trying to make him nervous. And it was succeeding admirably.

"I propose a partnership of sorts between the Assassins Guild and my organization."

"And what would my people get from such a partnership?" Bella asked.

Toole smiled at her. She had almost spit out the word *partnership*.

"You would get the elimination of the Thieves Guild, and control of the entire city. Is there more that you would expect?"

Suddenly, for the first time Bella looked slightly interested. One eyebrow raised just a fraction. If she had been a poker player, that would have been a deadly "tell."

"Look, Bella," Toole said, leaning forward and keeping both hands in plain sight on top of his desk. "I'm a businessman. I know business and how to make money and control this city with that money, from underneath and behind the scenes. I've proven that clearly to you and others over the past six months."

"Go on," Bella said.

"But I'm no good at the protection side. I've got a hundred men surrounding our position at this moment and I'm sure you and ten of your assassins could fight your way in here without the slightest problem."

"You are correct," Bella said.

"So," Toole said, giving her the palms-up gesture. "To stay alive, I need you. And to solidify control of the city, you need me and my organization."

"Assuming I agree with your assessment of the situation in this city, how do you see such a partnership working?" Again she almost spit out the word partnership.

Toole laughed. "I suppose partnership might have been the wrong term to use. You would be the leader, I would be your first lieutenant."

Again her eyebrow raised slightly and Toole knew he had her. So he pushed forward. "You run the city and protect me and my people while I do the finances. Within a very short time the mob and the Thieves Guild will only be a memory."

"And you will follow my orders?" Bella asked.

"My interest is business and money," Toole said, smiling at her while holding her stare. "As long as you protect me and my people, I'll follow you to the ends of the universe. And make you even more powerful at the same time."

Again her eyebrow raised slightly and Toole wondered if she knew she had such a clear giveaway of her emotions and thoughts. He doubted it.

She leaned forward, both hands on his desk. Her blonde hair fell over her right shoulder and he could feel the sheer power of her presence. "What exactly are you afraid of, Toole?"

He kept his gaze locked on hers. Then he sighed and shook his head. There was no point in lying to her. If what he proposed was going to work, she needed to know.

He took a deep breath and stood.

She also stood up straight facing him across the polished oak of his desk.

"Something is coming after me," Toole said. "I have no way of knowing what, or even who it is. But I know." He tapped the side of his head.

"And this *knowing* has you scared?" Bella asked. "Scared enough to give up control of your organization to me?"

Toole nodded. "Alive and second in command of the most powerful crime organization in the South is better than being dead." He laughed. "Actually it's better by a considerable distance."

For the first time since the most dangerous woman in the Big Easy had come though his door she smiled. "Mr. Toole, your organization and courage have impressed me for the last year. I will give your proposal some thought."

She offered her hand and he reached forward and took it. Her skin was firm and her grasp hard as iron. He returned her handshake, never taking his gaze from her eyes.

"I will leave a dozen of my people around your office, if you would like?" she said.

"That would be appreciated," Toole said.

"I will return this evening," she said.

Without another word she spun and started for the

door. Kyle managed to get it open before she got there, and she and her guard went through without so much as a squeak of the floorboards.

Toole let out a deep breath. "Kyle, make sure our people know they will be joined by some *professional* help."

"Yes, sir," Kyle said.

As the door closed behind Kyle, Toole dropped into his chair with a giant sigh. Then slowly, softly, he started laughing to himself.

So far, so good.

Over Toole's desk, Remy lay perfectly still, his ear pressed lightly against a small opening in the ceiling tile. He had managed to hear every word of the conversation between Bella Donna and Toole. And it had shocked him.

The Assassins Guild, to his knowledge, had never made a pact with anyone. And had no interest in controlling the business side of the crime world. Yet it was clear that Bella had liked Toole's suggestions.

If she took the alliance with Toole, there would be no doubt that the Thieves Guild would be in danger. The entire balance of power in New Orleans would vanish like steam above the Bananas Foster served in the Three Sisters Restaurant on Bourbon.

He listened as Toole laughed softly to himself. Clearly the man didn't need a lecture on the old ways of New Orleans. He knew them and was playing them against each other.

So what was Remy going to do now? His idea of dropping in on Toole for a lesson seemed pointless at the moment. He could drop down, take the guy out, and make his escape. But Toole was right. Someone else would quickly take Toole's place.

Toole stopped laughing to himself and stood. Remy moved slightly so that he could see down through a small crack down into the office.

Toole moved out from behind his desk, locked the door with a dead bolt, then went to the ornate bar. Quickly he picked up and set down six different bottles in succession.

There was a small click.

Right below Remy a panel opened on the front of Toole's desk.

Toole picked up and sat down three more bottles, then moved over to the open panel and knelt.

Remy could see Toole twisting what must have been the tumbler of a safe, then pulled it open. Toole reached into the open safe and pulled out a pouch of some sort, tied with a drawstring.

Toole opened the pouch and slid a large emerald out onto his palm.

Remy could hear Toole's sigh all the way through the ceiling.

"Okay," Toole said, his voice solid and fairly loud. "Come and try to take this now."

Toole held the emerald out in front of him for a moment, then slipped it back in the bag, put the bag back in the safe, and closed the panel door.

Remy just shook his head as Toole went back to the

bar and reversed his combination of bottles, then headed for the door to his office. A moment later he disappeared from Remy's view out the door.

What in the world was that about? Remy thought as he slowly sat up in the crawlspace.

CHAPTER 10

For the entire flight west Cain had sat silently, hunched over, staring out the front window of the X-Men's plane. He hated these wimpy, do-gooders run by his stepbrother. He was so used to fighting with them, that he almost considered lashing out at them right now.

But he didn't. Once before, they needed his help against Magneto, and he gave it because Cain didn't want to live in a world run by the so-called master of magnetism. This time, much as Cain hated to admit it, he needed their help.

From what he could tell by the pain in his chest, they had been right about where he had been heading. As the night wore on, it became very clear to him that he was still going in the right direction.

If it really was this Robert Service person who was causing his pain, he felt almost sorry for the guy. He was going to be nothing more than a smear on the sidewalk by the time Cain got through with him. And if there was another stone from the temple, Cain was going to own it, just so no one else would ever cause him this kind of pain again.

"Boise, Idaho," Summers said, pointing down at the city below and to the left of the plane. "Where Service spent the last part of the night."

Cain said nothing. He'd been thankful that Summers and his good-looking wife hadn't talked all night long. With the pain in his chest making him feel trapped, the addition of stupid small-talk from the couple would have made it impossible to keep from tearing their plane apart in midair. Then he would have been back to walking. Not that he minded walking, but this way there was a chance he'd get this pain in his chest stopped sooner, rather than later.

It just galled him that it was his stepbrother's little people that gave him the help. That he *needed* their help.

Suddenly the pain in his chest shifted. One moment it had been steady, then suddenly it was like someone was slicing a knife through his nerves.

He leaned slightly forward and stared out the window. Boise was behind them now. The source of his pain wasn't on the plane to Portland, that much was suddenly clear.

"Turn right," he said.

Summers glanced back at Cain, his visor giving the effect of being looked at with just one big eye. "What—?"

"*Right*," Cain said again, his voice a low growl.

Summers shrugged. A moment later the plane banked slowly right toward the south.

Now the pain got even worse.

"Other direction," Cain said.

Summers banked the jet back to the left, eventually heading north toward the mountains.

The pain eased back to where it had been all night.

Cain said nothing as both Summers and Grey glanced back at him.

After a moment Summers shrugged again and looked at Grey. "Guess we're headed north for a while."

"Guess so," she said.

Cain said nothing. There was nothing he needed to say to the idiots. As soon as he found what was causing his pain, he wouldn't need them anymore. And that wouldn't be a moment too soon, as far as he was concerned.

Finding the right valley in all the hundred of valleys had been surprisingly easy in a helicopter. Robert had kept the emerald tightly gripped in his hand and the moment the helicopter got slightly off course, he turned it back in the right direction. Craig, the pilot, had asked no questions as to how Robert knew when to turn, and in which direction. One of the advantages of overpaying for a service was that it always guaranteed a great deal of cooperation and very few questions.

And Craig was just about willing to do anything.

The helicopter flew over a low saddle and dropped down into the tree-filled valley below, skimming a few hundred feet over the pines as he went down. Above them the rocky tops of the mountains towered, littered with drifts of white snow even though it was the middle of the summer.

During the first ten minutes in the mountains, Craig's proximity to the trees had worried Robert, but then he'd settled into the movement of it and now understood it. There was no point in going any higher.

Robert pointed to the left over Craig's shoulder and Craig swung the helicopter in that direction, heading down the river that wound its way through the bottom of his narrow valley. Inside his head, Robert felt the feeling of correctness. This direction was right on the money.

And he was close.

Below them a clearing and a log cabin suddenly appeared, then disappeared behind them as Craig banked the helicopter to the left slightly to follow the river.

Instantly, the feeling inside Robert's head switched from right to completely wrong.

"That log cabin was it," he shouted to Craig. "Put the chopper down there." He pointed to a clearing a half mile down the canyon from the cabin. He'd go back to the cabin alone from there. No doubt the person who owned part of the emerald knew he was coming. And was going to protect the gem if he could.

Robert wasn't worried. Not in the slightest. It had taken him less than thirty minutes to find the gem in nine hundred square miles of wilderness. It was going to take even less time to secure it from whoever owned it.

Craig set the chopper down in the clearing with a slight bump, kicking up dust and pine needles with the wind from the blades.

"Keep it running," Robert shouted over the noise of the engine to Craig. "This won't take very long at all."

Craig nodded, then shouted, "Duck when you get out."

Robert only nodded and stepped out of the helicopter, keeping low until he was well away from the blades.

Then he stood up straight and at a quick run headed back up a dirt trail along the river toward the cabin. In his left hand, the emerald was grasped tightly. In his right, tucked into his jacket pocket, was his pistol.

THE JEWELS OF CYTTORAK

As he went around the slight bend in the valley and started up the trail toward the cabin, he slipped the emerald into his shirt pocket and buttoned it. He'd cut a small hole on the inside of the pocket so the surface of the emerald could be against the skin of his chest. It gave him power, and just in case he needed it, the emerald was there.

Then he slowed to a fast walk and put both hands open and above his head in the traditional sign of surrender. Ahead of him, he could see the old log cabin tucked against the edge of the steep canyon wall. In front of it was an open meadow leading down to the river.

Robert had no doubt he was now being watched, most likely through a scope. But he figured this person, whoever he was, would at least want to talk for a moment before he shot. And it was on that piece of human nature that Robert was counting.

Robert was within thirty steps of the small front porch of the log cabin when the door opened and a man with a long white beard stepped out. He looked to be in his late fifties and had dark, angry eyes. He held a rifle cradled across his arms, and as he stepped to the front of the porch he said, "You can stop right there."

Robert took two steps and halted, not more than six paces in front of the man.

"What do you want?"

"I've come to ask for your help," Robert said, keeping his hands in the air.

The guy's eyes looked at Robert. "You're a big fella. What do you need my help for?"

"I think you know," Robert said.

The old man stared at Robert, then looked away into the open meadow. "Yeah, I know."

Robert only nodded. "I could sense that you did. Do you know that something else is coming?"

The old man nodded. And for an instant there was a look of fear in the mountain man's eyes.

"That's what I need your help with," Robert said. "If we combine our gems, both touch both stones, then we might be able to stop this red *thing* that's coming. At least we'd have a fighting chance."

"And you expect me to just drag out my stone and give it to you?"

"No," Robert said. "I'll give you mine, first." Robert indicated his jacket pocket. "Can I bring it out?"

The old man nodded. "Real slow like."

Robert slowly moved his right hand down into his jacket pocket, then quickly yanked the pistol out.

The old man didn't have a chance. He didn't even get his rifle out of the crook of his arm before Robert caught him with two shots.

The gunfire echoed down through the valley, swallowed by the faint rumble of the idling helicopter.

The old man's rifle went clattering across the porch and down into the dirt as the he spun around and slammed into the logs of his home. Then slowly, a look of surprise on his face, he slouched to the wood of the porch.

"Sorry," Robert said, tucking the pistol back into his pocket. "Just didn't have any more time to talk."

With a slow turn he located the direction the stone was in, then started off toward the side of the mountain behind the cabin. Within a few seconds, he had narrowed the location down to an old stump.

Two seconds later, he pulled the second part of the emerald out of the small knot in the bark and into the air. It was a third of the size of the one in his pocket, but still beautiful in the morning sun.

He held it up with his bare hands as its energy flowed over and through him, making him feel stronger, bigger than before.

Suddenly his clothes felt tight as his strength grew.

And inside his head he could feel two presences. One weak and very far away, in the southern part of the country. The other huge and red and very close.

And the red one was very angry.

Robert slipped the second emerald into his shirt pocket and at a full run headed back down the trail toward the waiting helicopter.

As he climbed in Craig looked startled. "What happened to your clothes?" he shouted over the roar of the engine.

"I'm still a growing boy," Robert shouted back, then laughed.

Craig laughed with him as Robert pointed to the north down the valley away from the approaching red thing from the south.

"Keep it low to the river for a ways," Robert shouted to Craig, "then head straight for the McCall airport as fast as this bird will fly."

"Ain't got much choice," Craig said. "Dunno what you just did friend, but you weigh a helluva lot more. 'Copter can barely make it."

Robert just smiled.

• • •

Trying to track someone over the Idaho mountains with a small jet while being directed by the Juggernaut was not easy. And it was not something Scott had ever imagined he would ever be attempting.

From the moment they had crossed over the first range of mountains, Cain hadn't said a word. He'd simply sat hunched over in the back of the *Blackbird*, pointing.

First right.

Then left.

Then back right.

Scott had brought the jet right down as close as he could to the tops of the mountains, but even at that he had to keep them a good thousand feet up, which meant they were three or four thousand feet above some of the valley floors. Even another plane down there would be nothing more than a speck against the rocks and trees, impossible to see.

Twice the banking turns of the jet had overshot where Cain wanted them to go. The entire process was frustrating beyond belief. But Scott had no better idea on how to track Service, especially now that it seemed he had left his own jet.

He decided that they needed to take a more active role.

Activating the radio link, he said, "Storm, I want you and Rogue to start a more detailed search from the air. Take Wolverine with you, see if his enhanced senses can pick anything up."

"Suits me, boss-man," Logan said before Storm could answer. "Beats sittin' in this tin can."

"We shall do so immediately," Storm said.

A moment later, Scott saw the hatch on the side of the *Raven* open up. Storm flew out, gripping Wolverine by his wrists, borne on the winds she controlled. The hatch shut quickly. No doubt Ororo used her weather-working abilities to minimize the decompression in the *Raven*.

"They're away," came Hank's voice from over the radio.

"So I see," Scott said.

Suddenly Cain let out a loud grunt, then clinched his teeth and grabbed his chest as if having a heart attack. He growled like a caged animal ready to spring, so loud and so mean that Scott didn't know what to do. Being trapped inside the *Blackbird* with an angry Juggernaut was not something he ever hoped to experience. In fact, he'd been half worried about it all night.

Then Jean's thoughts came clearly into his mind. *Don't worry. I've got a telekinetic bubble around us just in case.*

Scott glanced back at where Cain still held his chest. For the first time Scott actually thought Cain was in pain. But how was that possible? The ruby didn't allow Cain to feel pain.

Unless the emerald was causing it.

"What happened?" Jean asked Cain. "Are you all right?"

"He got stronger," Cain said through clutched teeth. "Down there."

Cain pointed to a steep-walled valley with a river winding down the center like a small snake.

Storm. Rogue. Jean's thoughts were clear in Scott's head as well. *Check out the valley below.*

Jean nodded to their answers that Scott couldn't hear, then she turned to Cain. "Rogue, Storm, and Wolverine are checking out the valley. It will only take a minute."

Cain said nothing as Scott slowed the jet and put it into a tight banking circle pattern. Off to his right Hank did the same with the *Raven*.

"He's moving again," Cain said. "That direction." Cain pointed north down the river.

Scott swung the *Blackbird* out of the pattern and headed north.

Jean nodded to herself, then glanced at Scott. "We've got an old man shot down there," she said. "Storm says he's still alive, but aging before their eyes."

"Aging?" Scott asked and Jean only nodded.

"Beast," Scott said. "Got a medical emergency on the valley floor below. See what you can do to help."

"Understood," Hank's voice came back strong as the *Raven* turned and almost dove into the valley.

Scott glanced at Jean. "Have Rogue guide the *Raven* in. We'll continue after Service."

Jean nodded.

Cain simply pointed north.

On the ground below, Storm knelt beside the old man, then sat down on the porch and put his head in her lap.

He had been shot twice and they had found him on his back, on the wooden porch of his log cabin. He was alive, but from what Storm could tell, wouldn't be for long.

What was even stranger was that he seemed to be aging. When they'd first reached him, he had appeared to be a man in his fifties, but now he looked almost eighty and lines formed on his face as they watched.

Wolverine had let them take care of the man while he tracked Service's trail down the valley. Rogue had disappeared to guide Hank in for a landing.

Now the peaceful valley around the log cabin was shaking with the sounds of jet engines as Hank brought the small jet in for a perfect vertical landing on a flat area near the river. When he shut down the engines the sounds of the river slowly returned and the valley again seemed to be at peace.

Only a moment later Hank and Rogue were beside Storm and the old man.

Hank did a quick medical check, then shook his head at the same time as he dug in a small bag with one foot. "He's not going to make it," he said to Storm. "But I can give him something to ease his pain."

"Do it," Storm said.

Hank quickly injected the pain medication and after a moment the old man seemed to relax a little in her lap. Then his eyes fluttered and he opened them, staring up at her.

"I'm in heaven," he said hoarsely.

"Not yet," Storm said, slowly stroking the man's arm. "Rest easy."

He smiled at her. "So beautiful." Then he frowned

slightly. "Thought I could defend my stone." He laughed, then coughed, and a small trace of blood dripped from his mouth.

"Go easy," Storm said. She used her power to warm the area around him slightly as he shivered.

"Stone?" Hank said to the man. "Is that what Service wanted? Another emerald?"

The old nodded, never taking his gaze off of Storm's face above him. "Mine, his, and another. All part of one big stone."

Storm glanced up at Hank who had a worried look in his eyes.

Suddenly the old man started coughing. He now looked at least ninety, and his hair was falling out in Storm's lap.

He grabbed Storm's arm. "Don't take me off my land. Please? Promise?"

Storm nodded. "I promise."

A moment later, Storm could feel him relax.

And then he was dead.

Beside him Rogue stood and sighed.

Storm held the man's head for a moment, then eased it off her lap and laid it gently on the wood floor. Then she too stood, taking a deep breath.

"Didn't make it, huh?" Wolverine asked from the front steps.

"Did you find anything?" Storm said, turning to face her team.

" 'Copter landed down the valley," Logan said, "an' Service hot-footed it up here. Then he went to a stump near the edge of the slope back there. Somethin' was hid-

THE JEWELS OF CYTTORAK

den in there, somethin' that had a *nasty* scent, but it's gone now.''

"Another emerald," Hank said.

"Great."

"Hank," Storm said, "go back to the plane and inform Cyclops what has happened here. Then bring back two shovels. We need to bury this poor man."

"I'm not sure that's going to be necessary," Hank said, indicating the body of the old man. "My guess is the emerald gave him a very long life."

Storm was stunned. The old man's skin had already collapsed and dried in on the bones. And as she watched flakes of skin and hair blew away in the slight wind.

"Lordy," Rogue whispered.

"Inform Cyclops," Storm repeated.

Hank nodded and headed for the jet.

By the time he returned, the old man's bones were turning to dust and being scattered by the wind down his beloved mountain valley.

Storm's promise to him had been kept. He had stayed on his land and become part of it.

And five X-Men swore to themselves to get the man responsible for this and make sure he paid.

In the beautiful resort community of McCall, Idaho, Service barely squeezed aboard his private plane, smashing part of the galley as he did. After he got settled on the even-smaller couch, he punched the intercom button. "Get this plane in the air. And file a flight plan for Miami, Florida."

"Yes, sir."

Two minutes later, the private jet cleared the tops of the pine trees near the end of the runway and turned east, climbing into the clear blue summer sky.

Service wasn't paying any attention to the beautiful lakes and mountains below him. He simple sat on the couch and held up the two emeralds, turning them, studying them. After a moment he figured out how they fit together.

"One piece missing," he said to himself as he stared at the emeralds. "Just one. And that soon will be mine."

Then he laughed again.

CHAPTER 11

The attic area above Toole's office had become like an oven as the day went on. Remy was dripping sweat into the insulation above the ceiling tiles and the dust was sticking to him like gray paste. His hair was matted down over his headband and even the playing cards in the pocket of his duster felt damp and limp.

But like any good thief, he was a master at waiting. Didn't matter the conditions, he hated it. His normal inclination was to barge in fighting.

Fighting was easier. And quicker.

The outcome was determined almost at once.

Waiting was hard. But sometimes a good thief had to wait. And Remy was a good thief, maybe even the best there ever had been. And in this instance, waiting for Bella to return was the correct thing to do.

Above, he could hear the pacing of Toole's guards on the roof. Below, Toole and his thin assistant had come and gone from the office a number of times, but nothing Toole said indicated a change in the situation. Something was coming after Toole. Something he feared so much that he was willing to make a deal with the devil herself.

So Remy had waited. At times he could barely contain his desire to just drop into the room below and kick a few doors down.

But then the need for more information about Toole kept him in his spot.

And the need to wait for the return of Bella.

He waited and sweated and watched and listened.

Then around dinner time, things changed.

The door below slammed open and Toole stormed around behind his desk, sitting down hard in his big leather chair.

"Where is she?" Toole asked his assistant. "Whoever is coming after me is getting closer. And he's stronger. I can feel it. He's much stronger."

"She's left her people," his assistant said, obviously trying to calm his boss. "And more of them have arrived and taken up positions. They're guarding the building beside our men. No one can get in."

Remy didn't like the sound of that. Bella was up to something and chances were it wasn't a partnership with Toole.

"She had better not leave me out to dry," Toole said, sneering at his assistant.

"She won't," the assistant said.

"And you are correct," Bella said, her voice coming clearly to Remy's ears, even though she hadn't stepped in front of the desk to face Toole.

"Thank God," Toole said, standing to face Bella, who moved to face him. "I'm in great danger. Just since we last talked the force is close."

Remy's breath caught again in his chest. Here, right below him, was his wife, the woman he had loved more than any other. Yet she didn't remember her love for him. And now she had sworn to kill him if he ever returned to New Orleans. How surprised she would be to know her husband was above her at that very moment.

"I've thought about your offer," she said to Toole, coming right to the point.

"Yes?" Toole asked, the eagerness in his voice far too obvious.

"But first," Bella said, "I need to have three questions answered to my satisfaction."

Toole shrugged. "I'll do my best."

"First," Bella said. "The ghost sentries you employ around the Quarter. How is that done?"

Toole laughed and moved over to a picture on the wall. With a flick, he tapped a hidden switch and the wall slid back revealing a bank of screens and a half-dozen keyboards.

"Holographic projections," he said. "Hidden projectors in thirty places around the Quarter. We can project sound like voices and record at the same time."

Remy nodded. As he had figured. Nothing more than a security trick. A good one, for sure. It had kept Bella and her people as confused as it had Remy.

Toole tapped at a keyboard and then indicated a monitor. "For example, this person was asking questions about me the other night outside of the Bijou and we tracked him until he caught us."

"What?" Bella said, stepping toward the screen, the obvious surprise clear in her voice. "Idiot! Do you know who that is you tracked?"

Toole stared at her and even Remy could tell his jaw was open at being called an idiot by Bella.

"That," Bella said, pointing at the screen, "is Remy LeBeau. A thief."

Remy barely managed to not laugh. *Figures that Toole would show her that tape.* So, she was as afraid of him as he was of her. Good. Always nice in a marriage to have such mutual respect.

Toole shrugged. "So?"

Bella snapped around to the assassin behind her. "Have the building searched," she said. "Quickly."

Remy glanced around at the attic space. There was a small area up under a part of the rafters in the roof where he could hide just fine. But for the moment he was reluctant to move away from his spy post. Besides, it would take them a few minutes to find the utility tunnels and this attic space.

"Okay," Toole said, "what's your second question?"

"You said you're afraid of someone coming after you."

"Very," Toole said.

Bella nodded. "So what are you hiding that you're afraid to lose?"

Toole stared at her for a moment. Remy could remember what it was like to stare at Bella. He had done it often when they were together. But now, for Toole, staring at the head of the Assassins Guild must be a completely different matter.

"Nothing," he said after just one beat too long to make it convincing. "Whoever is coming, is coming for me."

Remy didn't believe him and neither did Bella, Remy was sure.

"Okay," Bella said, turning and moving a half-step to the assassin standing behind her. "Forget my third question. I've thought about your offer and I have an answer for you.''

As fast as a snake she took the sword of the assassin and swung around, cutting Toole's head cleanly off his body.

His blood spurted as his head went one direction and a moment later his body slumped to the floor.

Remy was slightly stunned. He had never expected Bella to join in a partnership with anyone, but the suddenness of her answer surprised even him. *Oh, well.* So much for his ''little talk'' with Toole about the customs of the old ways. It seems that Bella had given him a fine, and final, lesson.

Bella turned to the stunned Kyle. ''Unless you and the rest of Toole's men would like to end up exactly like your boss, I would suggest you get as far away from this building as you can, as quickly as you can.''

Remy could tell that Kyle didn't need any convincing. He nodded, swallowed hard, then backed quickly toward the door. At the door he turned and ran.

''Get everyone into positions,'' she said to the assassin she had borrowed the sword from. ''I want whoever is coming after our Mr. Toole here to walk into what seems to be a deserted warehouse. And no one moves until I say. Understand?''

The assassin nodded and left the room.

Bella kicked Toole's head out of her way, then went over to the wall of monitors. ''Well, well, dear LeBeau,'' she said, looking at the screen. ''You're in town. We just may meet again.''

Remy shook his head as Bella turned and left Toole's

office. If she only knew how close they really were.

He moved silently up and into the hiding place in the rafters.

One minute later an assassin moved quietly past where he had been.

Again, Remy went back to waiting. And this time he had no real idea what he was waiting for. He just knew that he and Bella waited for the same thing.

Whatever it was.

Scott landed the *Blackbird* next to the *Raven* in the large meadow, grateful as always for the craft's vertical takeoff/ landing capabilities that rendered taxiing unnecessary. He opened the hatch for the three of them to depart, but only Jean followed him out. The Juggernaut remained in his seat, hunched over, quietly growling. Scott had to hope that Cain wouldn't suddenly explode.

"What happened?" Scott asked Ororo as the X-Men gathered in a circle on the hot pavement of the airport. The only one who didn't join the circle was Jean, but Scott could feel she was listening through him.

"We couldn't find him," Ororo said. "His jet dropped off his filed flight path."

"Does he know he is being followed?" Bishop asked.

Scott shrugged. "Cain knows what direction he's gone, so it would seem logical that Service might know Cain is behind him."

"So we return to the original plan," Hank said. "We use Cain to track him."

THE JEWELS OF CYTTORAK

Ororo glanced at Scott. They were both team leaders, but for this mission she had been letting him take the lead. On missions in the past he had followed her lead. Sometimes it just worked that way.

"Storm," Scott said, finally deciding on the most obvious course of action. "You, Rogue, and Wolverine take the *Raven* and head south, see if you can pick up word of Service's plane on the radio. It's faster even than the *Blackbird,* and we'll have to proceed more slowly in case Cain forces us to change direction suddenly."

Ororo nodded.

"You're assuming, of course, that our Mr. Marko wants to remain with us," Hank said. "He's being uncharacteristically calm."

"At the moment he's using us," Ororo said. "The moment he no longer needs us, he'll be gone."

"We can only hope," Hank said, "to find Service before Cain reaches that point, or Service finds that next emerald."

Scott glanced at his watch. "Let's get going."

Robert Service stood in the humid afternoon heat of the New Orleans French Quarter, staring at the old warehouse. Other than a few people walking on the sidewalk down the block, and an occasional cab, the entire neighborhood looked deserted and mostly unused.

But Service knew the emerald he needed was in that warehouse. The third piece that would join with the two emeralds in his shirt pocket. He had no idea what would happen when all three were together again, but it didn't matter. From the moment he'd touched the big emerald in his father's room, he'd been driven to find the other parts.

And now his quest was almost finished.

After leaving Idaho, he'd had his pilots leave their planned flight path and go south toward Phoenix. Then, staying away from all commercial flight lines, and staying below ten thousand feet, they had made it into the south, at first heading for Miami, but then turning back when they passed New Orleans. In fact, spotting the emerald in New Orleans had been much simpler than finding it in the Idaho wilderness. And once on the ground, a simple cab ride had gotten him to the right neighborhood.

He glanced around. Nothing. No one watching, no one moving as far as he could see.

In the back of his mind the red creature was again getting closer. But it wasn't here yet. And whoever had last owned the emerald he was after had died earlier in the day. Service had felt it like a fleeting thought.

He moved across the street and toward what seemed to be the front door of the warehouse. He shoved it open, expecting resistance from a lock, or some sort of latch.

Nothing. The door had been left open.

Inside, the warehouse seemed empty, yet fairly clean. The air was a good fifteen degrees cooler than outside and the difference made small beads of sweat form on his arms and forehead.

He moved inside, strolling toward the back until it became clear in his head that the emerald was above him.

"Office upstairs, huh?" His voice echoed in the

empty space as he looked around, searching for a way up. A staircase against one wall seemed the best, and he quickly climbed them, finding a short hall and ornate office at the top. The door to the office was standing wide open and a decapitated man was sprawled on the expensive carpet, his blood now a dark brown stain covering a large section of the room.

"Previous owner of the emerald, I presume," Service said to the body.

He stood in the middle of the room and turned slowly, letting the direction of the third emerald show him the way.

The desk.

He stepped around behind the oak desk, but the direction changed. With a quick check of the drawers, he knew it wasn't in the desk.

It was in front of the desk.

Again he moved back around to the desk and the direction in his head said the emerald was very close. His mouth was almost watering at the nearness of his goal.

He bent down near the extended front of the desk and inspected the wood. A clear hidden panel.

Without a thought he smashed his fist into the panel, shattering the wood into splinters.

A small safe. He grabbed the handle of the safe with both hands and yanked.

An explosion sent him tumbling backwards, crashing into the bar. Except for the jarring of the impact, he felt nothing. No pain, not even shaken.

He quickly checked to make sure the two pieces of the emerald buttoned inside his shirt pocket remained against his skin in his tattered shirt. They were right where they belonged.

He stood and went back to the now-shattered desk. The door to the small safe was twisted and he yanked it off its hinges like tearing a piece of paper. He knew that he had gotten considerably stronger, but even that surprised him.

Inside the safe was a small leather pouch. He picked up the pouch and stood.

"I'll take that," a voice said from behind him.

He turned around to face a beautiful blonde woman in a purple outfit, flanked by two masked men carrying ninja-type swords. She stood with her hands on her hips, no weapon in sight. But from her attitude, it was clear to Service that she didn't think she needed a weapon.

He smiled at her. "Do you even know what's in here?" He held up the pouch.

"Something our Mr. Toole there," she gestured to the body, "was afraid to give up."

"As he should have been," Service said.

Holding the pouch carefully out in front of him so that she could see, he tipped it upside down and let the emerald slide out onto his bare hand.

The surge of energy, the blinding flash of green light, surprised even him.

And the feeling of power was so wonderful that all he could do was laugh.

Logan could smell the assassins hiding in the shadows of the old warehouse. He moved silently from shadow to shadow, working his way forward toward a side door. Service had gone in there, obviously not knowing he was walking into a trap.

And Logan wasn't about to stop him.

Not after following the guy around the entire country for the last day. As far as Logan was concerned, the ambush would do him some good.

An hour before, the *Raven* had picked up a radio request for an emergency landing for a private jet coming in to New Orleans from Idaho. Storm took the *Raven* there, radioing the *Blackbird* to do the same. When Hank pointed out that they could hardly land their craft in the middle of Jackson Square, they contacted the Professor. As it happened, there was, on the outskirts of New Orleans, a private airfield run by a young woman named Kris. She was a member of the underground network of mutants that the Professor kept in touch with. They could take in both craft without the difficulties that would arise if a group of outlaw mutants tried to land at a public airport.

Once they arrived, it was child's play for Wolverine to track Service's distinct scent to the warehouse.

Rogue and Storm were hanging back around the corner near a bar, letting him do the initial scouting. Rogue had tried to contact Gambit on the radio link, but he had turned his off. Neither Rogue nor Storm were particularly surprised at that, but it still would have been nice to have Remy along.

They had managed to then follow Service as he took a winding cab trip into the French Quarter, finally ending up in this old warehouse district. Cain and the rest of the

X-Men team should be landing at the airfield any time now.

Scott and Ororo had decided that the entire team should be together when they stopped Service. But as far as Logan was concerned, the guy would be easy to rail in. And if he got the chance, he'd do it. And get in an extra kick or two in reward for the hours crammed up in that plane.

Suddenly, from the second floor of the warehouse there was an explosion that rocked the neighborhood.

Logan smiled. *The fun's beginning.*

He moved boldly up to one of the masked guys with a sword who had been hiding in a small alcove near the door.

"Y' hear that?" he asked the guy.

Then, before he could even swing up his big sword, Logan flattened the assassin with a solid punch square in the cloth face mask. The guy dropped to the ground like a bag of flour.

"Been needin' to do that for days," he said, growling at the man slumped on the concrete. "Thanks."

Two more of the masked men faced off against him just inside the warehouse door. One smelled of garlic and needed a bath.

Wolverine charged right at them, ducking their wild sword swings and pounding his fists into the smelly one, then kicking the other into a backward flip.

The one who smelled of garlic scrambled to his feet and again faced Wolverine, sword ready.

"Anyone tell ya that y' smell, bub?" Wolverine said as he just walked right at the guy.

THE JEWELS OF CYTTORAK

The assassin raised his sword to swing and Wolverine hit him twice, so fast that the garlic man didn't even see the punches coming. The force of Wolverine's blows sent the assassin tumbling head over heels across the concrete floor of the warehouse. His sword clattered on the pavement like an alarm going off.

Four more of the masked men with swords stepped out of the shadows, facing Logan.

"Oh, now we're gonna have some fun."

Suddenly there was another explosion above him and the entire warehouse filled with bright green light.

"This ain't a good sign," Logan said, glancing around to see what had changed. Didn't look like anything had. At least not down here. Upstairs might be another matter.

Two more assassins stepped up to join the other four taking positions around him.

Six trained killers against just him. Was this for real or was he just having a wonderful dream?

Scott, Jean, Hank, and Bishop stood on the concrete taxiway where Kris had told them to park. In front of them, Cain slowly crawled from the *Blackbird*, finally gaining his freedom and standing. He did not look happy, but as far as Scott was concerned, Cain never looked happy. Scott was just impressed that Cain had stayed in the back of that plane as long as he had.

The humidity of New Orleans smothered all of them, a stark contrast from the dry heat of Idaho only a few hours earlier. And for most of the long flight from Idaho, Scott had worried about just this moment.

What would Cain do when they landed? Would Cain continue to work with them to find Service? Both he and Jean doubted it, since Cain never really worked with anyone. If they hadn't been offering him a ride, he wouldn't have even bothered to talk to them yesterday, let alone ride with them.

So what would Cain do?

Cain glanced at the four X-Men, then said, "What the hell're we waitin' for? We know where he is, let's get a move on."

Then suddenly Cain grabbed his chest and let out a yell that shook the ground and broke windows in nearby office buildings.

In less than two seconds the X-Men were beside him.

"Cain?" Jean asked, staring up at the pain-filled face of the Juggernaut. It was a sight Scott had never imagined he would ever see. Pain and the Juggernaut did not go together, unless it was the Juggernaut inflicting pain on someone else.

"He touched the other stone," Cain said, taking a deep breath and setting his jaw in a look of determination. "I'm gonna kill 'im for this."

Scott turned to Jean. "Can you take us to where Service and the others are?"

Jean nodded and formed a telekinetic bubble around the five of them, lifting and speeding them toward the French Quarter. Below them Scott could see the miles of distance between the airfield and the city. Above, he saw

THE JEWELS OF CYTTORAK

Jean's face furrow with the strain of lifting the Juggernaut's tremendous weight. But she could handle it.

She had to. They were about to meet their foe face to face.

CHAPTER 12

The first explosion rocked Remy as he lay on the thin, narrow walkway over Toole's office ceiling. Dust drifted down on him like someone had broken a bag of gray flour ten feet over his head. Twice he wanted to cough, but had managed to swallow it.

Below him he watched the huge man stand up after getting the explosion right in the face. He seemed to be unhurt and not much bothered by what would have killed any normal man. No wonder Toole had been so afraid of him.

The big man moved back to the safe and then ripped the door off the hinges, reaching in and pulling out the leather bag that Remy had seen Toole pull out earlier. The emerald in it must be something really special if it was getting this much attention.

"I'll take that."

Bella!

Remy eased forward slightly so that he could see where she was standing, facing the large man. She was flanked by two of her assassins, both with swords at the ready. She had no weapon in her hand.

The large man turned around to face her, then smiled. "Do you even know what's in here?" He held up the pouch for Bella to see.

"Something our Mr. Toole there," she gestured at the man she'd killed earlier, "was afraid to give up."

"As he should have been," Service said.

Holding the pouch carefully out in front of him so

that she could see, he tipped it upside down and let the emerald slide out onto his bare hand.

What happened next was not what Remy had expected.

The room exploded, as if another bomb had been set off.

Remy held his balance on the board as it bounced and shook, then he quickly went back to watching what was happening below him.

Bella and her two guards had been blown back against the wall. They looked stunned, but alive.

A bright green light radiated out from the large man like he'd suddenly been turned into a huge, powerful spotlight.

And as Remy watched the man got even larger, slowly taking on the proportions of—

Suddenly Remy understood what he was witnessing.

The birth of a second Juggernaut.

The emerald was like Cain Marko's ruby.

Two Juggernauts in the world. Not good.

Not good at all.

Where were his X-Men teammates when he needed them?

Finally the green glow stopped.

The man stood at least seven feet tall, his head brushing the high ceiling just below where Remy crouched. His muscles were huge and his clothes hung off him in tatters. The emerald was a gigantic, glowing jewel in the center of his chest, attached there by a force Remy could only guess at.

Suddenly the building shook and again dust rained

down on Remy as the behemoth started to laugh, flexing his muscles, staring at his own hands and arms.

One of Bella's assassins swung a big sword at the laughing giant, but the blade just bounced off him.

Without missing a laugh, the man flicked the assassin away, knocking him clear through the wall and into the next small office.

And that seemed even funnier to the man, so he laughed even harder.

Bella, along with the other assassin, did the smart thing. They got out of there, ducking through the door while their opponent was still in a good mood.

Remy had no doubt that was the last time he was going to see her anywhere near this new Juggernaut. Fighting straight up, something as big as this man had become, was not her Guild's style.

Another time, Bella, Remy thought as his wife disappeared toward the stairs.

On the main floor of the warehouse, between laughs from below, Remy could hear fighting breaking out. He had no idea what was going on down there. Maybe some of Toole's men were too stupid to run and were attacking the assassins. The assassins would make quick work of them.

Remy scrambled quickly to his feet, then aiming at a panel near the door below, he dropped through, crashing to the floor of the office and tumbling once toward the door leading to the stairs.

He came up on one knee, facing the huge man with the tattered clothes, the emerald in his chest, and the hearty laugh. From this angle, Remy was now sure that he was as large as the Juggernaut. Not good.

Not good at all.

"Where did you come from?" the man said, his voice booming so loud it smashed the last remaining monitor on Toole's ghost setup.

"From your worst nightmare, *mon ami*." Gambit quickly charged two cards and in rapid succession flicked them at the behemoth. He wasn't sure how effective they would be, but he had to at least give it a try.

The explosions rocked the building, and made the man pause for a moment, before taking another breath and continuing to laugh.

But nothing else.

The explosions hadn't even staggered him.

Not good.

This was not good at all.

Wolverine kicked hard at two of the assassins surrounding him, sending both tumbling backward over the concrete as a dozen more assassins swarmed down the stairs from the second floor, led by a beautiful woman in purple.

Behind them, from the second floor, someone was laughing really, really loud. An annoying laugh that almost broke into Wolverine's good mood.

Almost, but not quite.

He spun and interrupted another assassin's sword with a sharp punch to the guy's face. He could feel his nose snap. Blood instantly flooded the inside of the assassin's cloth mask, soaking it, and dripping down the front of his chest. He stood there for a second in what seemed to be a frozen shock, then slumped to the floor.

Again the laughing from upstairs rolled through the warehouse like thunder on a hot summer day.

"Someone's havin' more fun than me," Logan said, growling at the ceiling.

Behind him Storm and Rogue arrived.

Around him, out of the shadows, dozens and dozens more assassins swarmed at him.

Rogue immediately went to work on the masked figures, sending them flying in all directions.

Storm spun up a small tornado and took out four more, smashing them back into the wall, leaving them there, stunned and without swords.

Wolverine, between slashes with his claws at the sword arm of one assassin, and kicking another in the gut, saw the woman in purple, flanked by two of her troops, slip out the back door toward the river.

"The boss lady just cut outta here," Wolverine shouted to Storm. "Want me t'go after her?"

"Our primary concern is Service," Storm said as she struck two of the assassins' swords with lightning, charging them enough to force them to drop the weapons. That set them up for Rogue.

"Just thought I'd ask," Wolverine said. Then with three quick slashes, he cut down three of the assassins as above him two more quick explosions rocked the building.

"A real war zone," he shouted to Rogue, who only nodded as she snapped the heads of two assassins together.

Down the stairs near the door Gambit bounded, taking the stairs three at a time. About halfway down Gambit dove and rolled, coming up behind a large cement pillar. Then, with three quick flicks of the wrist, he sent a card sailing back up the stairs. Those cards of his were more powerful than hand grenades, and about a million times more accurate.

Three more explosions rocked the building.

More laughter filled the warehouse.

"Remy!" Rogue shouted with a mixture of elation and concern.

"Joinin' the fun, bub?" Wolverine asked as he dove in beside Gambit to avoid the flying wood and concrete from above.

The Cajun actually looked surprised. "What are you—"

At that moment Wolverine glanced up at the huge, almost naked figure of a giant coming down what was left of the stairs. *This*, he thought, *has gotta be Robert Service.*

Gambit charged a large chunk of wood and tossed it at the giant as Service reached the bottom of the stairs.

Wolverine ducked behind the pillar with Gambit just as the explosion rocked the warehouse. This one actually made the big guy take a step backward. Then he stopped, glanced down at the tattered remains of his clothes, and laughed again.

"Annoying, ain't he?" Wolverine said.

Service cut off his laugh and started toward Gambit and Wolverine.

Both of them stood, side by side, ready to fight. Wolverine had his claws out, Gambit had cards charged and ready to toss.

Wolverine was ready for this fight. Service had been the reason for that long trip around the country. Now he was going to pay the price.

And as far as Wolverine was concerned, the fare wasn't going to be cheap.

Suddenly the two of them were picked up and wisked almost instantly back across the warehouse floor by Rogue.

She sat them both down. "Sorry, Storm's orders." Then she smiled at Gambit. "Hi there, sugar."

"Good t'see you, *p'tite*," Gambit said, smiling back at her.

Behind them Service laughed and started toward them.

"You two lovebirds mind?" Wolverine said. "We got a fight to finish." He stepped over the body of an assassin to meet Service head on. No matter what the size, he wasn't afraid of anything.

"Wolverine," Ororo's voice cut through the warehouse. "We work together on this."

Logan stopped, growled, then nodded, staring down the approaching giant. After being cramped up in that tin can for so long, this was what he was spoiling for. But Ororo was right. This was a teamwork situation all the way.

Beside him Gambit stepped forward and stood his ground beside Wolverine.

Storm moved to the far right.

Rogue went left, staying beside Gambit.

Wolverine let his claws snap outward, then smiled at the approaching giant.

Explosions were rocking the warehouse as Jean released the telekinetic bubble around the four X-Men and the Juggernaut just outside the door. Scott went through the door first, ducking left, as Bishop came in behind him, going right.

The warehouse looked as if the fight had been going on for some time. Bodies of masked figures were scattered around the concrete floor. Some still had swords in their hands, others didn't. From what Scott could tell, they were members of the Assassins Guild. But what that guild had been doing here was anyone's guess at the moment.

Wolverine, Rogue, and Storm had been joined by Gambit and were in the process of facing down the huge Robert Service. There was no doubt that now he was as large as the Juggernaut, and the emerald had attached to him and was glowing from his chest.

In the past the team hadn't had a great deal of luck beating the Juggernaut, but they had managed to stop him at times. And the way Scott figured it, Service wasn't as experienced a fighter as Cain, and was still new to the powers.

And he wasn't protected from Jean's powers by a helmet like Cain wore.

So maybe they had a chance.

"Now," Storm shouted to her team.

Wolverine and Gambit charged. Gambit threw a half-dozen cards in quick succession right at Service's bare chest.

At the exact same moment Storm hit him with a full bolt of lightening.

Instantly, it seemed, Rogue and Wolverine were at Service's feet, snapping them out from under the behemoth, sending him over backward with a huge, earth-shuddering crash that smashed the concrete under him.

"Phoenix!" Scott shouted. "Can you get through?" He hoped that she could use her telepathy on Service and bring him in under their control.

Jean was standing, concentrating, shaking her head. She glanced at Scott. "The two jewels are connected in some fashion," she said. "It's creating a nasty psychic interference. I can't break through it."

Scott frowned. "All right, we'll try a more direct approach."

With Jean at his side he stepped forward and fired at Service, carefully adding his optic blasts into the fight, making sure he didn't hit any of his teammates.

And for the moment it looked like they actually might beat Service.

Then, like a monster raising up out of the ocean in a late-night B-movie, Service stood up.

With a swat he sent Wolverine sailing through the air and squarely into Bishop. Then both of them smashed into a cement support pillar. The impact would have killed any normal human, but Wolverine was back up almost instantly and headed once more for the fight.

Bishop was a little slower getting back to his feet.

Service took Rogue's grip on his leg and bent back

her hand until she let go, then shoved her so hard that she went through the roof. A block later she managed to get control and return.

Service then gut-punched the Beast off his back, turned and hit the returning Wolverine so hard it smashed him through the roof. The Beast skidded across the pavement for a short distance before snapping himself up and around. Bishop tried to help Beast, but a backhand by Service sent him flying again. The blow knocked him completely senseless and by the time he came to, the fight was over.

Service ignored Scott's blast and Storm's bolts, walking right at them, forcing Scott to back up and finally move aside.

Wolverine came back for a third time and hit him again, full in the head, claws slashing.

Service again just flicked Wolverine away, this time sending him through a wall and out into the street.

Gambit picked up a large chunk of concrete, charged it, and tossed it directly into Service's chest.

The explosion blew out one wall of the building and shattered windows across the street. Jean barely got a bubble around herself, Ororo, and Scott to protect them from the blast.

But Service seemed completely unfazed. Scott was amazed. So soon after getting the gem Service seemed as powerful as the Juggernaut.

Ororo then tried one more trick. As Service stepped past Scott, she covered him with a quick cloudburst, then froze the water instantly on him and around his feet.

That stopped him for all of two heartbeats. Then the ice on him cracked.

After that, he clapped his hands.

The impact resulted in a shockwave that sent the X-Men flying.

As the mutants tried to pull themselves together, Service stomped one huge foot down on the floor. The ceiling came crashing down around them.

Then the world went black around Scott Summers.

The pain in Cain's chest felt like it used to feel when his dad hit him hard, with the belt. In all his years as the Juggernaut, he couldn't remember pain like this.

As a kid, he couldn't get away from the pain. His father's belt was like a constant reminder. But as the Juggernaut, he'd escaped the pain. And no one could push him around. Now, suddenly, the pain was back.

And he felt trapped with it.

So, as he did when he was a kid, stuck with his father and that weakling stepbrother Charles, he got angry.

Angry at being trapped with the pain.

Angry at the pain.

And even angrier at the cause.

Service had taken out the X-wimps before Cain even had a chance to get near him.

Which suited Cain fine. It meant Cain had Service to himself. "I'm gonna kill you now," he said.

Service just laughed.

Cain hated being laughed at. Nobody laughed at the Juggernaut.

He started to walk forward. The floor planks strained under his weight.

"Funny thing about these warehouses," Service said. "They're very old. And with a very weak structure. Why, I bet it would take just one impact in the right spot—"

He stomped his right foot onto the already-strained floor.

Suddenly, Cain felt the ground give out from under him and he fell.

"Happy landings!" Service called down, then laughed again.

Cain fell through to a basement, landing on a concrete floor. He didn't feel the impact.

He did feel anger.

He started to search for a way out of this basement. Then he'd find Service.

It didn't matter how long it took.

And when he did, his green glow would be painted all over the pavement.

Rogue smashed her way through the rubble of what used to be the warehouse ceiling before finally reaching daylight. Whatever this Robert Service guy was like before, she thought, he was definitely in Juggy's class now.

She looked around to try to find her teammates. At first, she saw nothing, but then a red optic blast came flying upward through the debris. Scott, Hank, and Bishop climbed up through the hole the blast had made. Seconds later, several bits of ceiling seemed to move of their own accord, which meant Jean was at work. Logan, Jean, Gambit, and a shaken-looking Ororo surfaced after that. Rogue remembered Storm's claustrophobia and shivered. Being buried alive like that must have been torture for her.

"Everyone all right?" Scott asked. After various affirmative grunts, he asked, "Where's the Juggernaut?"

Logan said, "He bolted. So's Service. I got both their scents. Follow me."

The Canadian mutant led the team through the streets of New Orleans—where, Rogue noticed, the pedestrians barely batted an eyelash at the gaudily dressed super heroes, three of whom were flying through the air.

As they moved, they noticed evidence of Service's passing: smashed cars, broken lampposts, and the like.

"That ain't Service," Wolverine said. "That's Marko. He's followin' our man."

"We're heading back the way we came," Bishop said. "Toward the airfield."

Sure enough, they arrived shortly at the airfield. Service's trail had gone cold, according to Wolverine, but Juggernaut's trail led right to the *Blackbird*. Which sat by itself.

"Where's the li'l Shi'ar ship?" Rogue asked.

"Good question," Scott said, sounding more than a little testy.

"Mr. Summers!" called a female voice. "Thank God you're back!"

Rogue turned to see a short woman with brown hair trailing out from under a Twins baseball cap. It was Kris, the owner of the airfield. She didn't look like a mutant to Rogue—but then, someone who just met Rogue wouldn't think her to be one, either. She wondered what the young airfield owner's powers were.

"Kris, what happened?" Scott asked. "Where's the *Raven*?"

"The Juggernaut stole it."

Gambit groaned. "Well, ain't *dat* jus' fine?"

Kris shrugged. "He just stomped in, climbed into the *Raven*, and took off. We couldn't stop him."

"I hope you didn't even try," Scott said.

"How'd the big lug even know how t'*fly* the thing?" Rogue asked.

"Fairly easily, actually," Hank said. "Like the Danger Room upgrades the Shi'ar provided, the *Raven* uses a telepathic interface. Pretty much any idiot can fly it just by thinking about it. And Cain isn't just any idiot."

"Service probably took off in his own plane and Cain is following," Ororo said.

Logan snorted. "Good bet."

"Then we'd better follow both of them," Scott said. "Let's go, people."

As one, the X-Men moved toward the *Blackbird*. As they went, Rogue wondered how much good it could do. Robert Service had already beaten the X-Men once, without even working up a sweat. They weren't likely to do any better the second time.

Still, they had to try. That's what being an X-Man was all about.

Gary Service had just finished looking in on his father, then had returned to his office, when his private phone rang.

He had hardly slept at all the night before, and had only catnapped as the day had progressed, and he'd heard no word from anyone. It had been one long day.

He'd managed to track Robert's plane to Idaho, then back to New Orleans. But he had no idea what was happening. The old man was alive and looked like he would be for days, if not weeks or months. So what happened to Robert was critical to Gary's plans. And even though he hated his brother, there was a small part that was worried about him.

Gary quickly picked up the phone before the second ring and simply said, "Yes."

"Gary Service, please," a voice said. "This is Hank McCoy."

"Yes, Doctor, this is Gary. Any word on Robert?"

"Not good, I'm afraid," McCoy said. "Your brother managed to find the other parts of the emerald."

"Other parts?" Gary asked, shocked. "So that's what he was looking for. What did the gems do to him when he touched them?"

"Remember the picture of the Juggernaut you found?" McCoy asked.

"He's like that?" Gary asked, even more shocked. The Juggernaut, from all the accounts, was an unstoppable force. There would be no fighting Robert if he got like that.

"I'm afraid so," McCoy said. "And he's heading back your way right now. His ETA is about three hours."

"What?" Gary couldn't keep his voice from shouting into the phone.

"Our plane is faster, so we should be arriving shortly

before he does.'' McCoy hesitated. ''And Gary—he's killed at least one person that we know of.''

''You can beat him, though, right?'' Gary asked, the hope again gaining strength.

''We don't know yet,'' McCoy said. ''But we need to do something before the Juggernaut catches up to him. He's between us and your brother.''

''Oh,'' Gary said. Now his head really was spinning.

''My suggestion is for you and your father to *not* be there when we arrive.''

''I think,'' Gary said, ''that I will take that suggestion. Thanks.''

''Good luck,'' McCoy said and hung up.

Gary dropped the phone back in its cradle, then leaned back, forcing himself to take deep breaths. Robert had turned into another Juggernaut.

He had killed a man.

And he would be home within hours.

Gary pounded his fist on his desk. What was he going to do? It felt as if the end of the world was at hand. All his years of planning, of gaining control of his father's estate, would be wasted. His dream of using all of his father's dirty money to give to charities would be lost.

Lost in one day. All because of a stupid emerald.

Robert would kill him when he learned what he had done, or at least force their father to sign it all back over to Robert. If Robert really was the size of the Juggernaut, there would be no fighting him.

Then suddenly Gary laughed. *Wait, you idiot*, he said to himself. *Robert killed a man. If he can be reverted back to a regular human, he will spend the next twenty-years-*

to-life in prison. And Gary would be free to give away the old man's money as he pleased. Maybe this dark cloud had the old silver lining after all. If Robert could be stopped.

But not even the Beast was sure he and his people could stop him.

Gary suddenly had a clear plan, as if it had been there all along. He had three hours, which gave Gary barely enough time to get everything fixed. Maybe, just maybe, this might turn out to be all right. If he was lucky, and could prepare fast enough.

Gary quickly stood and headed back for his father's room. As always, the smell of rotting flesh greeted him twenty paces from the door.

Gary smiled at the nurse who was sitting near the door of the room, reading. "We've got a problem," he said. "We've got to move my father out of the house as quickly as possible. Anywhere away from here will be fine."

The nurse, a large woman with thick, solid arms, frowned, then said, "Andreassi Memorial Hospital's closest."

"Good. Call for an ambulance."

She reached for the phone while Gary moved over beside his father, who slept fitfully.

"Father?" Gary said aloud. "I'm afraid we've got to move you to a new location. Before Robert returns."

The old man slept on, half snoring, half choking.

Gary stared at the rotting face of his father. The man's sickness had been appropriate for the way he had lived. Maybe he should just leave him for Robert. But still, the man was Gary's father and Gary had to protect the changes in the will, just in case Robert couldn't be beaten. He wondered if there was a jail cell that could hold Robert, if he was the size of the Juggernaut.

"Sorry, Father," Gary said. "But we've got to be going." He nudged the old man gently under the sheet.

The nurse talked quietly for a moment on the phone, then hung up and turned to face Gary. "They're sending an ambulance. It will be here in ten minutes."

"Good." Gary looked at the rotting skin on his father. Gary felt bad having to move him, yet it had to be done.

"Father," Gary said, a little louder. "Time to wake up."

Suddenly his father coughed, then sighed.

And stopped breathing. Just like that.

The heart-monitoring machine screamed into a long, high-pitched call of alert.

"I just tried to wake him," Gary said, more for himself than the nurse.

She moved over beside the bed and did a quick check, then reached over and turned off the machine. "Nothing you did," she said. "It was just his time."

Gary nodded.

He stood for a moment, staring at his father's body. Having the old man gone was such a relief. Gary almost felt embarrassed that he was feeling that way standing over the man's death bed. Almost.

Now Gary just had Robert to deal with.

He turned to the nurse. "Cancel the ambulance."

The nurse nodded and smiled. "I'll take care of getting your father's body to the funeral home and getting this room cleaned up a little.''

"Thank you," Gary said. "I appreciate it." He turned and headed back to his office. He had a lot of people to inform, business transactions to complete in only a few short hours.

And he had a few other calls to make. If the super heroes couldn't handle Robert alone, maybe he could help a little. Now that he had the money.

Then, after Robert was locked away in jail, Gary would start giving his family money away. Slowly, but surely. Every last cent of it. It would be the least he could to repay the world for his father's greed.

And the sins of his brother.

CHAPTER 13

Outside the Xavier Institute for Higher Learning, the sun was starting to set, and the air remained thick, hot, and humid. In the cooler interior of the mansion's study, Professor Xavier hovered in his floating chair near the door and reached out telepathically to the X-Men as they winged their way northward in the *Blackbird*.

The most palpable sense was fatigue and discouragement. They had hauled Cain around the country trying to catch Robert Service. And they failed to do so before Service killed one man and was transformed into another Juggernaut-like creature. Then Service had beaten them rather soundly in a fight. Xavier sensed failure and frustration hanging heavy in the *Blackbird*. It was not a feeling these X-Men were used to.

As Phoenix brought him up to date telepathically— including Gambit's own adventure with Wingate Toole, the Assassin's Guild, and Service—the Professor shuddered. Service had killed the man in Idaho in cold blood, and probably would have done the same to Toole had the Guild not beaten him to it. Cain Marko having the power of the Juggernaut was bad enough, but Cain was basically a bully and a thief. Service was an order of magnitude worse.

He had to be stopped.

So for now the question was how to handle Service. And the Professor needed his team thinking, not of the failure of the last day, but of the future.

There was also another factor he feared: What would

be the results when the two jewels were together? Touched by the same person? He had a few theories, and none of them were good.

The Juggernaut's and Service's power came through the jewels from the bands of Cyttorak. It was as if the jewels were funnels, focusing the power of Cyttorak into this world. But if the jewels were together, controlled by only *one* person, there would be no telling what kind of destructive force could come through into this world.

The Professor closed his eyes and relaxed, using his own mutant abilities to send out mental probes that would allow him to mindlink with his students. Instantly, he felt the presence of all seven X-Men, as if they were in the study with him.

Cyclops was the first to "speak." *Do you have any recommendations as to how we should proceed, Professor?*

"In fact, I do, Scott. For one thing, I believe we should concentrate on doing everything in our power to keep Cain and Service apart."

Why? Rogue said. *Seems the two of them beating on each other might be the best solution.*

"Perhaps. But I fear the consequences of the two jewels coming together."

As do I, Hank said. *Those jewels are basically windows into another dimension. We don't want that window opened any farther than it already is.*

"We can't afford to take the chance," the Professor said, "if we can stop it."

He felt the impact of his words on his team. The entire group seemed to stiffen, sit up straighter at the challenge. They were tired, hungry, and beat-up. But the nature of who they were always brought them up for the good fight.

We have two advantages, Scott said. *We know where Service is headed, and the* Blackbird *is faster than his plane. We can arrive at the estate ahead of him. The other advantage is that Cain* doesn't *know where to go. All he can do is follow where the ruby tells him, but that isn't precise. It should buy us some time.*

The Professor nodded. "I agree, that is the best course of action. Cain's delay in arriving should give us time to find a way to revert Robert Service to his former self."

Wolverine laughed. *We ain't had much luck doin' that to Marko.*

"No," the Professor said, keeping his voice from showing the disappointment he felt over that very subject. "But Robert Service has one weakness that Cain does not have."

The stone, Hank said, already clearly following what the Professor was saying.

"Exactly," the Professor said. "The emerald was in three pieces and did not initially attach itself to him. Cain's ruby was always intact. We need to return the emerald to its broken state."

We have considerable power at our disposal, Storm pointed out. *Perhaps if we focus our energies in one blast on the emerald, we can shatter it.*

I can work on him telepathically, too, Jean added. *He doesn't have the protection Cain has—no helmet. But Cain's presence will ruin that. Once the ruby gets too close to the emerald, the psychic interference is too much for me to overcome.*

"It's a start," the Professor. "Godspeed, my X-Men."

Charles Xavier sat once again alone in his library, and he worried. Even with the *Blackbird*'s speed, it would be at least an hour before they reached the Service estate. This break would also allow him to do some research into this problem. And right now it just might be any little detail that would spell the difference between success.

And unthinkable failure.

On the *Blackbird*, Rogue looked over at Remy. He looked like hell. He had taken a moment at the airfield to wash the worst of the dust off his face and purchase a fresh deck of cards from Kris—the old set had gotten moldy— but his duster and costume still were almost caked with dust.

But weirdest of all was the smile Remy had on his face. Where the other X-Men looked tired, or had expressions of grim determination, only Gambit looked pleased.

"Sugar, you sure do look happy for someone who just got his butt whupped."

"*Cherie*, 's far as ol' Remy is concerned, it's mission accomplished. De rest is jus' cleanup."

"Cleanup? How you figure that? We still got us *two* Juggernauts t'deal with."

Remy laughed. "I went back home 'cause t'ings was

goin' wrong. Well, de cause o' dat was Wingate Toole, and *il est mort*. And de source o' his power is takin' up residence in *M'sieu* Service's chest. So t'ings should be goin' back to normal."

Rogue shook her head. "If y'can call Thieves Guilds an' Assassins Guilds normal."

"Well, as normal as dey get in N'awlins, anyhow," Remy said with another laugh.

"I'm jus' glad you're okay. Even if you do look like a human dust bunny. Do me a favor, don't go harin' off to a place where they wantcha dead by yourself again, okay?"

"It's a deal, *p'tite*. It's a deal."

Cain sat in the tiny chair at the front of the *Raven*. He wondered where his stepbrother got his hands on a ship like this. Probably that alien chick he was sweet on. She'd rebuilt the mansion for him when it had been destroyed, so it figured that she'd give him ships like this one.

Cain liked it. All he had to do was think a direction, and it went. Sweet. Real sweet.

He'd been flying northeast toward New York. Summers had mentioned that Service's estate was in central New York, and he could feel himself getting closer to Service the closer he got to that state.

Perfect.

Soon the pain would be gone. Cain was going to enjoy this.

• • •

It was shortly after one in the afternoon when Scott brought the *Blackbird* into a soft landing on the edge of the Service estate private runway.

This time no one came out of the shadows to greet them. Scott sincerely hoped that Gary Service had taken his advice and left. Service's little brother in the middle of the fight was the last thing they needed to worry about at this point.

Beside him, Scott could feel that Jean really didn't want to be back here. Their last experience with the dying old man had not been pleasant. Scott didn't want to be here, either.

"Don't think about it," Scott said, grinning at her and patting her hand.

"Easy for you to say," she said, smiling back. In his mind the words, *I love you*, formed.

"We gonna sit here all day?" Wolverine asked.

"Sorry," Scott said. He released the side door, letting in a wave of humid, hot air.

One by one, the eight X-Men exited the plane. Wolverine lead the way through the heat toward the large main mansion.

As they got closer Wolverine stopped and sniffed the air. "Smells like something died in here."

"You might say that," Scott said.

Around them nothing was moving. On this hot, summer afternoon, even the birds seemed to have found a place to hide.

"Anyone inside?" Scott asked Jean.

She shook her head no. "Totally empty, from what I can tell."

"How long until Robert Service arrives?" Bishop asked, staring at the building, then scanning the grounds.

"From what we can figure," Scott said, "within the hour."

Jean nodded and focused off into the distance while Scott glanced around. "We should set up out here to make our stand."

Bishop spoke up. "With respect, Cyclops, I disagree. We should take the battle inside."

"Inside?" Scott asked, surprised at Bishop's suggestion.

"Explain," Storm said.

"Since Service owns this building, he might hold back on damaging his own property. Also, inside, his increased size will put him at a disadvantage in movement in the comparatively cramped indoors. Plus, we can use the natural lay of the rooms to our advantage."

Scott nodded, and looked to Storm, who did likewise. His natural inclination would be to stay outside, but this time Bishop's logic sounded right. Still, he didn't want to put all the eggs in one basket.

"Storm, take Gambit and the Beast and guard the front of the house. The rest of us will guard the rear. If Service arrives first, we go back to the main plan and attack the emerald on his chest with everything we can throw at him. If we break that thing off him, all our problems are solved."

"And Cain's also," Hank said.

"If Cain arrives first, we shall endeavor to keep him away from Service, at least until the emerald is destroyed," Storm said.

Scott nodded. "Good. Inside, then."

CHAPTER 14

The red creature felt very close, but still south, as Robert Service's plane landed at the family estate's personal runway. Another jet sat to one side of the runway. The same one that had been in New Orleans. Somehow it had gotten here before him. More than likely it belonged to those annoying mutants he'd crushed in the warehouse. Didn't matter to him one way or another. He'd just flick them away like flies, then get to business.

He taxied the plane inside the hangar and squeezed out, managing to not damage the plane too much.

The first order of business was his dear old father. His fondest hope was that at the sight of his new size, his father would have a heart attack and die. That would make the day perfect. Otherwise Robert would just have to kill the old man. Not anywhere near as much fun as scaring him to death.

Then Gary would most likely run away, to never return and that would make it even better. Could he be that fortunate? Could he scare his father to death and have his younger brother disappear, all on the same day? Over the last two days he'd been very, very lucky, so the chances were good.

Very good.

He laughed and his laugh echoed through the trees of the estate on the hot, summer afternoon. It felt good to be home.

He went around the side of the hangar and headed for the house, going in the back way. He cut through the kitchen and into the large dining and formal living room area. The picture windows were open, an attempt to alleviate the awful stench of his dear father's disease, which permeated the whole house.

The room was huge. There were many times his father had entertained fifty people here. How small the place seemed now. What had once felt like a gymnasium-sized area now seemed small and cramped. And he had to duck to get through every door.

Near the dining room table stood two of those mutants he'd been fighting in New Orleans. One had a single-visor lens over his eyes and the other wore a skintight yellow and blue outfit, with long red hair streaming down over her shoulders.

"You people," Service said, "should really learn to mind your own business. Now get out of my house." His voice shook the room and a picture dropped off of one wall.

"Don't think so, bub," a feral-looking man in yellow and blue said as he moved around the dining table to come in from Service's right. Behind him was a huge black man with an "M" tattooed on his face.

In the doorway beside the woman with red hair, another woman entered with a green and yellow body suit on, with a brown flight jacket over it. A white streak ran down the center of her brown hair.

Then a black woman literally flew in through the open window. She wore a silver-black bodysuit and had striking white hair flowing down over her shoulders.

"Ready?" the man with the glasses asked.

"For what?" Service said. "I said get out of my

house and I'm not going to warn you again. What I did to you in New Orleans will seem like child's play."

"Ready," all three women said.

"Now."

A red bolt of energy shot out from the visor and hit Service square in the chest.

Service staggered more from surprise than anything, then stood his ground, feeling the energy flow into his body.

Lightning shot out from the black woman, also striking him in the chest.

More energy flowed into his emerald and then into his body.

Again he staggered, but held firm, staring at his attackers. They would not even move him. He would show them.

The woman with the red hair strained, as if her efforts were taking their toll.

Inside his head Service could feel a tickling sensation, but nothing more.

"Is this all you have?" he asked, then laughed.

"Not quite," the woman with the white streak in her hair said.

Suddenly she shot forward, head down, and rammed him in the chest.

It felt as if the world had exploded around him.

He went flying backward, smashing through the dinning room wall and into the kitchen as darkness flooded over his mind.

This can't be happening, was his last thought.

• • •

Cain headed the craft in sharply toward the private runway behind a large estate. He was really getting the hang of this plane. Think left, the plane went left. Think right and the plane went right. Made flying a whole lot easier.

He stared at the tree-covered estate below. All he wanted was to get on the ground as quickly as possible. He could tell that Service was down there, in that big house. He was going to finally catch up to the guy and really pound him. Hard.

Payback for all the pain. And for leading him clear around the country, making him work with the X-Men again.

Cain focused on getting on the ground and the plane followed his thoughts, tipping nose straight down, heading directly for the large hangar.

"Hey," Cain said, "not so steep!"

But it was too late. He had focused on getting on the ground for too long and the plane had responded. Taking him to the ground.

Straight at the ground.

Fast.

With a huge impact and explosion, the plane smashed into the hangar, and the jet inside. A huge fireball roared into the air. Twenty miles away the ground shook.

It took Cain thirty seconds to push his way up out of the flaming wreckage. He emerged unscathed. He shook off debris, stood, and headed for the big mansion.

"Nothin' stops the Juggernaut, pal," he said to the big house. "'Bout time you found that out."

• • •

"De big guy," Remy said, staring out at the huge fireball from the direction of the runway, "has arrived."

"I was wondering how he was going to do on landing," the Beast said. "I see he did it in normal Juggernaut fashion. Too bad. That was a good little plane."

"Here he comes," Gambit said.

The Juggernaut was striding across the lawn. And Gambit could tell he was angry.

Very angry.

A large explosion shook the center of the house.

"Looks like dis up t'me an' you," Remy said.

"Seems that way for the moment," the Beast said. "Until the others finish their task of breaking up that emerald."

Gambit stepped to an umbrella stand near the back door and grabbed all four umbrellas and the walking stick that it held. Then he went through the back door and out onto the lawn, the Beast right behind him.

The Juggernaut saw them and only shook his head, not slowing down in the slightest.

Gambit hadn't expected him to.

"Stop dere, *mon ami*," Gambit said.

The Juggernaut said nothing. Just kept walking.

Remy charged the first of the umbrellas with kinetic energy and then threw it like a spear at the Juggernaut.

It hit, tip first, on the Juggernaut's chest and exploded.

One right after another Remy charged the umbrellas and threw them.

One right after another they exploded against the Juggernaut's chest.

And one step after another the big guy kept coming. The explosions didn't even slow him down.

This was twice in two days Gambit had faced one of these big monsters. It was getting old real fast.

Hank then bounded right into the Juggernaut's path. "Cain, listen to me. You have to give us a chance to stop him before—"

The Juggernaut didn't even let Hank finish talking. He swung at the blue-furred mutant with a giant fist. Luckily, the Beast had been expecting it, and managed to duck the blow.

"Okay," Hank said, leaping to the roof of the house in a single bound. "I've always felt that violence is the last refuge of the incompetent, but if it's fisticuffs you want, then it's fisticuffs you'll get.

He ripped apart a brick chimney and threw each brick with uncanny accuracy, using both hands and one foot. The bricks hit the Juggernaut like machine-gun bullets, one right after the other against his head with intense force.

He didn't even glance up.

Gambit grabbed a small lawn statue of a frog, charged it with energy, and threw it as hard as he could. The explosion against Juggernaut's chest blew out the windows in the kitchen and back area of the house.

But Cain Marko was obviously too angry to even stop and fight. He just kept going.

He reached the back door of the house and didn't even bother to open it, just plowed right on inside.

Gambit glanced up at Beast on the wall of the house and shrugged.

"Let's hope," Beast said, "that our friends were a little more successful than we were."

Gary Service pointed to the driveway to his estate. "In there."

He held on as the driver of the camouflaged transport truck turned sharply and sped up the driveway. A huge fire was raging behind the mansion, near the runway. Gary didn't want to think about the chance that was Robert's plane burning back there. He wanted his brother stopped and in jail, not dead.

The transport truck skidded to a halt in front of the main door to the mansion and a moment later a second truck did the same. As Gary climbed out twenty men jumped down and formed two lines, facing the mansion. Each man wore military garb and were armed with knives, hand grenades, and AK-47s. It was the largest force Gary could put together in the few short hours, and it had cost him over a quarter of a million to do it. But if it helped capture Robert, it would be worth it.

"Half in the side door," Gary said, pointing to his right. "The other half come with me in the front."

Explosions rocked the ground. It sounded to Gary as if they came from behind the house.

Trager, the man in charge of the mercenaries, quickly had his men running in both directions as Gary moved up and shoved open the front door.

Inside smoke drifted in the air in the marble foyer. Crashes and small explosions echoed from the direction of the kitchen. *Sounds like there's a war going on in there*, Gary thought.

"This way," he said, heading down the hallway, ten armed and trained men right behind him.

Cyclops bent over the still form of Robert Service. The emerald was still attached to the man's chest and he was starting to stir. They clearly hadn't been able to damage the stone enough to break it free. But it was clear that the stone was divided into three parts. Just how to break the gem back into those parts was the main question.

And there wasn't much time from the sounds of the explosions rocking the building from the back. The Juggernaut was almost here and there was no telling what he would do when he found Service.

Cyclops glanced around at Phoenix. "Can you get a mental lock on him?"

After a moment she said, "No. The interference between the two gems is fierce."

Service groaned.

"What knocked him out?" Rogue asked.

Before Cyclops could respond, the outside wall of the kitchen exploded inward, covering them all in flying dust and wood.

The Juggernaut had arrived.

He stopped just inside the kitchen and looked around through the dust. "Where is he?"

THE JEWELS OF CYTTORAK

"We've got to keep them apart!" Cyclops shouted. "Storm, lay down an ice path back toward the runway."

Instantly Cyclops fired his hardest ray square at the Juggernaut's chest as Storm created a blizzard of snow and freezing rain to cover the ground under the Juggernaut with a sheet of slick, smooth ice. The room grew significantly colder, and Cyclops noticed the sun disappearing behind a sudden influx of clouds.

With a rolling tackle, Wolverine knocked the feet out from under the Juggernaut, sending Cain sprawling on his back on the ice and snow. Then the force of Cyclops's beam pushed hard, sending the Juggernaut back along the path that Storm was laying down.

Gaining speed away from the house.

After the Juggernaut was moving at a good clip, completely unable to stand or stop on the icy surface, Cyclops stopped firing his beam. The momentum of the Juggernaut might carry him for a mile or so, as long as Storm kept the microblizzard going.

On the floor in front of him Robert Service moaned and tried to sit up.

"Anyone got any bright ideas?" Wolverine said, looking down at the huge form of Robert Service.

Before Cyclops could answer, a large group of men carrying guns charged into the dining room and took up positions, weapons aimed at the X-Men.

Then Gary Service stepped forward.

And Robert Service stood up.

• • •

The Juggernaut had never been as angry before as he was right at that moment. He felt like a turtle trapped on his back, sliding, unable to stop. That and the intense pain in his chest from being so close to the man with the green emerald. He was almost clear back to the runway before his anger moved aside and allowed him to think. The X-Men had tried this stupid stunt on him once before.

He slammed his fist hard into the ground, right through the layer of ice.

Instantly he stopped.

He stood by stamping his feet hard, down into the ground below the layer of ice. Then he turned and headed back for the mansion.

Storm flashed ahead of him and back inside before he had taken three steps. It didn't matter. This time he would take care of that stupid Service and stop the pain.

And Charles's little scout troop wasn't going to be able to stop him.

"Gary," Cyclops shouted. "Stay out of this! X-Men, ready!"

He poured his hardest beam straight into Robert Service's emerald, just as they had done before.

Bishop yanked out an electrical socket, touched the two wires together against his palm, and directed the electrical charge at Service's emerald.

Storm dropped in beside Cyclops and added her strongest bolts of lightning.

This time Service stood there laughing.

Cyclops couldn't believe what he saw. It was as if Service was taking all the energy being shot at him and using it to get stronger.

Suddenly Rogue, head down, flashed at Service. But this time he was ready for her. He simply raised an arm and smashed her aside, sending her through a wall and off into the air.

"Halt!" Cyclops shouted and cut off his beam. Bishop and Storm did the same with their attack.

An odd silence fell over the crowded dining room, kitchen, and hallway area.

Then again Robert Service laughed, the huge sound echoing through the house.

"Anyone ever talk to you about that annoying laugh, bub?" Wolverine said, sneering.

Hank, who had entered with Gambit a moment behind the Juggernaut, shook his head. "This is not a good development at all. Not at all."

"Got dat right, *mon ami*," Gambit said.

Service ignored the X-Men, and the men with the rifles. He faced Gary Service. "Nice seeing you again, little brother. How's our dear old father holding up?"

Gary moved one step toward his huge older brother and stopped. "He's dead."

Robert Service again laughed. "I knew I was having a good day."

"I'd say that good day is about to end," the Juggernaut said from the hole in the side of the kitchen where the door used to be.

"So," Robert Service said, turning to face the Juggernaut. "You're the red creature who has been following me and causing me such pain."

"Stop him!" Gary shouted to the men with the guns. He pointed at the Juggernaut.

Instantly the room was rocked with the intense noise of ten AK-47's opening fire at once.

Cyclops knew that to the Juggernaut, those bullets were nothing more than annoying little bumps. The bullets ricocheted in all directions off the Juggernaut, tearing up the walls and ceiling of the kitchen.

Phoenix instantly formed a telekinetic bubble around the X-Men.

Dust and plaster filled the air along with the incredible sound of ten AK-47 rifles being fired inside at the same time.

One man with a rifle went down, a small hole spurting blood from his arm, the result of a ricochet.

"Hold your fire!" Cyclops yelled. When it became clear that the men had no intention of doing so, he shouted to his team, "Get the guns away from them!" Another ten armed men stormed into the crowed area, filling the area with chaos.

The Juggernaut stepped two huge steps forward and grabbed Gary Service. He held Gary out in front of him like a rag doll in the hands of a child.

Wolverine meanwhile slashed through two of the rifles with his claws. Then he took the two men and cracked their heads together.

Beast, using both hands and one foot, yanked guns out of three others' hands.

Shouting, "Leave my brother alone!" Robert Service

jumped forward into the line of gunfire that still raged at the Juggernaut, smashing a huge fist into the side of the behemoth's head.

The blow caused the Juggernaut to drop Gary. Storm whisked the dazed man out of danger with a gust of wind as she blasted three other guns with lightning.

Less than a minute after Cyclops had given the order to disarm them, the firing stopped. Every man with a weapon had been stripped of his firepower.

Wolverine snarled at two of them. "Get out of here before I tear you apart and have you for dinner."

"It would not be unwise to heed my friend," Hank said, twirling one rifle with the toes of his right foot. "He loves red meat."

Without waiting for orders from their leader, or Gary, the men scrambled for any opening they could find out of the area.

As they did so, Robert Service hit the Juggernaut with a huge, solid blow to the chin.

It was a blow Cyclops could imagine no one surviving.

The Juggernaut flew backwards, crashing through the wall and landing on his back on the lawn.

"This is going to be fun," Service said, stomping after him through the hole.

Cyclops glanced at his teammates. The fight they had hoped to avoid was about to happen. And there didn't seem to be a thing they could do about it.

• • •

Robert Service felt stronger than he'd felt all day. He stomped after the big red man. Just like his green emerald, Robert could feel that this man had a red ruby embedded in his chest. And Robert felt a huge desire to take that ruby. It was like a hunger, an addiction he couldn't control.

He would own that ruby or die trying.

The red man stood and stomped at Robert.

The two met solidly, and Robert knew instantly as he reached for the man's chest, that this guy had as much strength as he did. He peeled back the Juggernaut's armor to reveal the ruby.

At the same moment the Juggernaut reached for the emerald on Robert's chest.

As Robert's hand touched the ruby it felt as if the world had opened up to him. His strength a moment before was nothing compared to what he would have when he possessed the ruby.

But at the same moment the Juggernaut touched his emerald and Robert felt his very life force being pulled through the emerald and into the body of the Juggernaut.

With his free left hand he smashed at the Juggernaut, but couldn't dislodge him.

One of them had to win. Only one could possess both gems. And he would be the one.

The Juggernaut smashed at Robert's head with his left hand, while holding onto the emerald with his right.

But Robert held on and hit right back with his left hand, never letting go of the ruby with his right.

The energy flowed into his body from the ruby and

drained out at the same time through the emerald.

Then back around again as they hit and hit and hit.
Neither winning.
Neither losing.

CHAPTER 15

Back in the Xavier Institute, the Professor frantically worked at the mansion's Shi'ar-built computer. At the moment he wished Hank was there to help him. But he didn't have the time to recall Hank. He had to do it himself.

Since the last report from the team, he had hurriedly worked out and ran a dozen computer simulations of what would happen when Robert Service and the Juggernaut met. Over the years, with the help of others, he had studied the power and details of the ruby on Cain's chest. He had dozens of copies of various texts filled with tales, legends, histories, and religious tracts. He also had them scanned by the alien computer so they could analyze the data more thoroughly than any human mind. Even a mind as impressive as Charles Xavier's.

He had originally gathered all this information in the hopes of some day finding a way to return Cain to normal. Now he used it to try to stop a madman.

The computer simulations did show one clear result immediately. If one person held both the ruby and the emerald in their possession, that person would be a factor of hundreds of times more powerful than the Juggernaut. Such a person could rule the world.

Or destroy it.

No force would be able to stop him from doing either.

Now, today, those two stones were coming together and somehow, there had to be a way to stop either Cain or Robert Service from gaining control of both stones. And gaining that incredible power.

Somehow the Professor knew that the solution to all this was in the emerald. It had been broken into three parts at some point in the past. It could be broken again. But his problem was to find out how before it was too late.

If it wasn't already.

Gary Service slowly came to. His head hurt and he felt as if someone was sitting on his chest.

He last remembered the Juggernaut picking him up, strong hands smashing the wind out of him.

Then Robert had stepped forward and hit the Juggernaut. And that was the last he remembered.

His brother had saved his life.

Amazing.

Gary moved on the soft sofa and a sharp pain shot through his side. He must have at least two ribs broken. Slowly he forced himself to sit up, the pain taking his breath away and causing his eyes to water. But he had to see what was going on.

Outside explosion followed explosion. Something was still happening, that was for sure.

But for the moment his biggest concern was what had happened to his brother.

Phoenix stood with the other X-Men in a circle around the two battling giants on the green lawn of the Service estate. The day had been hot and sticky, but Storm's microblizzard had reduced the temperature significantly.

The battle, however, had heated things up tremendously. The energy flowing from them ionized the air, forcing the X-Men to slowly back up, giving the two standing giants more and more room.

Phoenix focused her mind. The two gems caused psychic interference locally, but it didn't seem to hinder long-range telepathy. She called out to the Professor.

I'm here, Jean. The Professor's voice came back clear in her head. *And I see what's happening. You must get them apart if you can. I need more time.*

We'll try.

Phoenix turned to Cyclops. "The Professor says we must get them apart. He needs more time to find a solution."

Cyclops frowned, staring at the two battling giants. Phoenix knew that the wheels had been turning in Cyclops's mind since Juggernaut and Service started going at it. "Can you put a telekinetic shield between them the moment we do?"

Phoenix nodded. "Not likely to hold them long—especially with the interference." She knew it wouldn't hold them at all, and she knew Cyclops understood that. He knew the limits of her power almost as well as she did.

"It will if we keep them busy," Cyclops said, reaching over and gently touching her hand in support. "We can only hope that the time we manage will be enough. How long did the Professor say he needed?"

"He didn't," Phoenix said. She smiled at the frown

on her husband's face. She knew the X-Men were facing as hard a task as any they'd faced. Of all their foes, Juggernaut had proven the most difficult to defeat.

"X-Men!" Cyclops shouted. "Gather around."

A moment later the various X-Men stood around him. Phoenix studied the combined team.

Gambit looked dirty and tired, his brown duster streaked with black. She couldn't remember ever seeing him look so disheveled—and, for Gambit, that was saying a lot.

The Beast stood beside Gambit and kept studying the two giants, frowning, as if looking at a giant puzzle.

Storm looked unruffled and calm, as she always seemed. Rogue, on the other hand, looked quite ruffled and not at all calm, her white-streaked hair in bad need of combing. A large smudge of dirt marred one cheek.

Bishop and Wolverine stood side by side, also a stark image of contrast. Bishop stood like the perfect warrior, straight-backed and showing no emotion, while Wolverine crouched like an animal, a snarl firmly in place.

"The Professor wants us to get them apart as quickly as possible," Cyclops said.

Storm nodded in agreement. Phoenix knew that was the signal between the two team leaders as to who would take command in this instance.

Cyclops returned the nod. "First," he said, "we have to blow them apart. Then Phoenix will put up a telekinetic shield between them."

"That won't hold them if they make a concerted effort to break it down," Hank said. "And from what they are doing at the moment, it seems likely that they would."

Phoenix nodded. She knew that also.

"Understood," Cyclops said. "That's why we have to keep them from making that effort in any fashion we can. What we're after here, people, is to buy time. As much as we can.

"Bishop, I want you to thrust your hands into that energy field that building around the pair of them. That should short them out for a moment, and also charge you up. Rogue, once they're distracted, I want you to smash into Service at the exact same moment that Storm and I hit the Juggernaut with everything we've got. Aim at the left shoulder. That should add extra torque and spin them. That should be enough to knock them apart."

"Agreed," Storm said, nodding.

"Once they're apart," Cyclops said, "I want Storm, Rogue, and Bishop to keep Service busy. The rest of us will do the same for Juggernaut, while Phoenix keeps up the telekinetic shield any time they start at each other. We keep that up until the Professor contacts us."

All the team nodded.

"All right," Cyclops said. "Take positions."

The X-Men fanned out around the fighting giants.

Phoenix moved so that she was standing on a line that she hoped, in a moment, would be between the two. Bishop took up position in front of her.

Scott and Storm faced the Juggernaut behind Service.

Rogue floated a distance off behind Juggernaut, facing Service.

"Bishop, now!" Cyclops shouted.

The mutant from the future leapt forward, and thrust his fists into the ionized air around the two combatants.

Phoenix smiled a grim smile and prepared her telekinetic shield. As Cyclops had hoped, Bishop's sudden intrusion distracted both Service and Juggernaut for a moment.

"Go!" Cyclops cried.

Almost instantly, Phoenix saw Rogue flash at Service. His left arm was in the air, preparing to hit the Juggernaut. She hit him solidly, head down, square in the left shoulder.

At the same moment Cyclops and Storm blasted the Juggernaut in his left shoulder with as much power as they could muster.

The sudden and surprising impact sent the two giants flying apart, head over heels through the air.

Phoenix almost wanted to clap for joy. The first part of the plan had worked even better than they'd hoped. The two were far enough apart that she didn't need to put up a shield.

Service smashed into the side of his mansion and disappeared inside in a large cloud of dust and shattered lumber.

Cain landed a half a football field away on the wide lawn, crashing into a large oak tree as he came down.

"X-Men," Cyclops shouted, "keep 'em busy!"

Phoenix stood her ground as Wolverine, Beast, Gambit, and Cyclops headed across the lawn at the Juggernaut.

In the other direction, Rogue and Storm flashed inside the house, joined a moment later by Bishop.

The fight was on. Phoenix just hoped it wouldn't be their last.

• • •

Cyclops watched as the Juggernaut climbed back to his feet. He was angry, more than Cyclops had ever seen him before. And they had seen him angry—Cain was not one to hide his emotions.

Wolverine was first to arrive near the Juggernaut, who started back toward the mansion. Wolverine came in fast and hard, clipping the part of Juggernaut's chest, just under the ruby, that was exposed by Service's rending of his armor.

The impact caught the Juggernaut in midstride and knocked him off his feet. Perfect flying tackle, except that Wolverine didn't get out of the way fast enough and Juggernaut smashed him aside, sending Wolverine flying into a nearby oak tree.

Cyclops watched Wolverine hit and crash through the branches. He hit the ground and lay still for a moment, then slowly climbed back to his feet. There was no one tougher than Wolverine. He would be all right.

Gambit peppered the Juggernaut with exploding cards square in the eyes and chest as he tried to stand up. Even the Juggernaut had to hold up his hand for protection as hand grenade-sized explosions went off in his face, one right after another.

"The ground!" Hank shouted, pointing at the lawn in front of the Juggernaut.

Cyclops understood. Under Cain's feet he blew a hole in the lawn. Caught off-balance by the explosion, the Juggernaut toppled into the hole.

"Keep digging!" Hank shouted.

Cyclops focused his hardest and tightest beam at the bottom of the hole, moving it quickly back and forth, blasting away huge chunks of the earth under the Juggernaut and deepening the crater.

"Don't stop," Hank shouted. "It's working."

Cyclops kept the beam focused, going down, deeper and deeper, as the Juggernaut fought to grab a handhold, anything.

"Gambit. Help me dig!" Cyclops shouted as the pit reached twenty feet deep. Focusing his beam this intently was starting to give him a headache, and the help would be appreciated. Besides, Juggernaut was too deep for Gambit's exploding-cards-in-the-face trick to be effective any longer.

"And blow the earth away from his hands," Hank said, "to keep him from climbing."

Instantly Gambit switched his aim, tossing one kinetically charged card after another at the ground under the Juggernaut as Cyclops continued pommelling the dirt and rock.

Every time Cain managed to grab a hand- or foothold, Gambit blew it out from underneath him. It was as if he was on a huge, exploding slide leading directly into the bowels of the earth.

In all their years of fighting against the Juggernaut, this was the first time they had tried this trick as far as Cyclops knew. For the moment, it looked as if it was working.

"Bête," Gambit shouted over the sounds of the explosions coming from below, "I only got fifty-two o'dese t'ings. Remy, he need some ammo."

Beast instantly scrambled toward a flower bed nearby. Then with expert aim, he used both hands and one foot to lob rocks, the rubble of small statues that had been smashed in the fight, and bricks back to Gambit, who caught them, charged them with kinetic energy, and tossed them with deadly aim into the pit below.

Cyclops figured the hole they had dug was at least a hundred feet deep and thirty feet across when he shouted, "Stop!"

He cut off his own beam, then tried to study the bottom of the pit through the smoke and steam.

From what he could see, Cain stood on the bottom, staring upward.

"You're dead, Summers," the Juggernaut said, his huge voice rumbling out of the ground like it was coming from a gigantic megaphone.

"Y'look good down there, Marko," Wolverine said, walking up and staring down into the huge hole.

"You won't look so good when I get out of here."

"I'm waitin'," Wolverine said, smiling.

The Juggernaut growled and started back up the side of the hole, pounding his fists and arms into the sides of the dirt for handholds.

Cyclops was amazed at how quick he was moving. It was easy to forget that the Juggernaut was fast, given how massive he was.

"Gambit," Cyclops said. "Let's keep him down there. You take his right side, I'll take his left."

"Bête," Gambit said, "keep de ammunition comin'."

Cyclops blasted the side of the hole under the Juggernaut's left foot while Gambit blew away the ground under his right.

With a growl the Juggernaut tumbled back to the bottom.

Cyclops blasted the pit another ten feet deep under the Juggernaut, just for an extra margin of safety.

As the dust and steam cleared, Cyclops watched the Juggernaut stand and start up the side again.

Rogue and Storm found Robert Service near the front door of his mansion. The momentum from Rogue's hit had sent him crashing through three rooms. He was just starting to get back to his feet as they flashed into the room.

"You'll pay for that," he said, "as soon as I finish with that red beast."

"I'm so worried," Rogue said, smiling at Service and slamming into him as he was starting to rise, knocking him to the floor again. She flew off before he could get his hands on her. She figured that if she got Service angry, he might go after her instead of Juggernaut. Not likely, but worth the chance.

Service tried to clamber up once again, but a hurricane force wind smashed into Service's chest.

Clearly Service hadn't been ready for that.

Storm's gale knocked Service over backward and through the front wall of his home as if it were so much tissue paper.

Halfway down the driveway he landed and skidded, then managed to stand and stay standing against the combined force from the two women.

THE JEWELS OF CYTTORAK

Service staggered two steps forward at the sudden stop. Both women floated between him and his mansion, smiling.

"That was fun," Rogue said. "What's next?" It actually had been fun. She enjoyed seeing someone like Service, who thought they were all powerful, get their just desserts.

"Twister," Storm said.

Rogue knew instantly what she meant. They had pulled the same trick on the Juggernaut a number of years back.

"Laugh all you want," Service said. "But you will—"

He took a step toward the two women and Storm lowered the temperature, bringing the blizzard back, forming a thick sheet of ice under his feet while Rogue rushed at Service's right side.

The big guy moved to hit her, but she knocked his arm away, sending him spinning like a top on the sheet of ice.

Storm kept the ice thick under him while Rogue spun him.

And spun him.

"Heck, sugar," Rogue said, laughing, "you're makin' me dizzy just watchin'." Sometimes, she thought, this job was actually fun. And spinning a killer like Robert Service was about as much fun as she could have. She just hoped Remy and the others were having as good a time pounding on the Juggernaut out back.

Service spun for a good fifteen seconds, during which time Bishop finally caught up and joined the group.

Then Service dropped to his hands and knees and smashed one fist through the ice, instantly stopping his spinning.

Rogue was impressed. It had taken him almost a full minute less than the Juggernaut to figure out the same thing. Finishing this guy off was not going to be easy.

When Service looked up at the three X-Men his face was red, his eyes bulging.

Slowly he climbed to his feet as the color returned to his face, replaced by the pale intensity of anger.

"He seems upset," Rogue said, her tone laced with mock concern. "Normally he's such a happy-go-lucky sorta guy. Always laughin', an' all."

"Just keep joking," Service said between gritted teeth. "I will have the last laugh when this is finished."

Rogue smiled at him sweetly. She would do everything in her power to keep him distracted from the Juggernaut. And making him mad at her was one way that seemed to be working just fine.

Storm looked at him sternly. "I doubt that. You have killed a man in cold blood. You will be punished."

Service only snorted, then started back toward the house and the Juggernaut beyond.

"I have an idea," Bishop said. "Rogue, bring me those power lines."

Rogue knew what Bishop was going to try. "And do a little wrapping along the way?" she asked Bishop.

Bishop gave Rogue a sharp nod.

A moment later Rogue had the hot power lines off the nearby poles and in her hands.

"A little water and ice, Storm," Bishop said.

Service was shortly drenched in water and the ground under him still layered in thick, hard ice.

As fast as she could go Rogue spun the thick, charged wires around Service.

Then she handed the hot end of the wires to Bishop. He held the wires with his left hand, channelling the charge through himself and blasting it—along with the energy he'd accumulated from Service and the Juggernaut earlier—back at Service. Again, he focused on the emerald. Rogue nodded in appreciation. There was still a chance, after all, that they could break the emerald in three. If they did that, it would make things much easier.

Service's hair stood directly on end from the charge and his face turned red as he strained to break out of the wrapped wire.

Then, with an angry roar, Service did just that. A shower of sparks flew in all directions. Storm moved herself out of their path. Neither Rogue nor Bishop bothered doing the same. Her invulnerability protected her, and his mutant power allowed him to absorb the charge.

"You don't look so good, sugar," Rogue said cooingly to Service.

"Can you get him airborne?" Storm asked Rogue.

"I can try."

At full speed she headed off to the side of Service, then came around behind him faster than he could follow and hit him low and upward, square in the back of his legs.

It felt as if she'd run into a solid stone wall. The impact rocked her.

Her blow sent him about ten feet into the air.

Instantly a tornado formed under him and spun him upward.

Rogue landed next to Bishop and worked to catch her breath. That impact had almost knocked all the wind out of her and she felt the impact clear through to her bones.

"Are you all right?" Bishop asked.

She nodded and took another deep breath. "Just give me a half a minute before you ask me to run. That's what I get for bein' cocky 'bout bein' invulnerable."

For thirty seconds Storm kept Service spinning in the air. Then the big guy tucked his arms tight against his side, put his legs together, and twisted around slightly so his legs were aimed at the ground. There just wasn't enough surface on him for the winds to hold that much mass aloft.

He hit the ground like a missile, going up to his ankles in the concrete.

"Now," Service said, stepping out of the hole he'd made and glaring at the X-Men. "If you are finished playing around, I've got a red monster to deal with."

He turned and strode toward the mansion.

Rogue glanced at Storm. "I got an idea that'll put some distance 'tween him and here," she said. "Gimme a boost?"

Storm nodded.

With a quick turn Rogue spun around and came in at Service low and upward. She caught him right in the center of his stomach, pushing upward and away from the Service estate with everything she had. She could feel the boost of Storm's winds helping her lift him.

One hundred feet.

THE JEWELS OF CYTTORAK

Two hundred feet.

She could feel his hard hands grabbing her by the shoulders like steel vises and yanking her away from his body. Then as if she were nothing more than a rag doll, he physically threw her aside.

She tumbled through the air for a moment, then righted herself and turned to watch.

Storm's winds kept pushing on Service. For a few more moments Storm managed to shove him higher and farther away from the mansion. If he'd allowed it to continue, Rogue had no doubt that Storm might just have given him enough velocity to reach orbit. Maybe even beyond.

But again Service didn't let their trick last long.

He simply pulled in his arms tight against his body again, and then put his legs together. With a simple twist he aimed for the ground.

Nothing Storm could do at that point. His huge body was like a wing cutting through the air. So she stopped and with Rogue returned to the front of the mansion.

By the time Service hit the ground in the middle of a nearby forest, he was almost a mile away from the Service estate.

Storm turned to Rogue and Bishop. "Let's retreat and make a stand where Phoenix has her shield," Storm said. "I don't think we can do much more out here."

"Over the top," Rogue said, holding out her arm for Bishop to hold onto. "Need a lift?"

A moment later they landed beside Phoenix.

"We stopped him for a short time," Rogue said to Phoenix. "But he's headed back here."

"Not long enough," Storm said.

Rogue could only nod her agreement to that.

For a short time Cyclops thought that just maybe they had found a way to stop the Juggernaut. He kept trying to climb out of the huge hole they'd dug under him, but every time Cyclops and Gambit had simply knocked the Juggernaut's hand- and footholds away.

"Cyclops," Hank said, pointing back toward the mansion. "Storm and the other team are beside Phoenix. It would appear they might need some help with Service."

"Wolverine, go and see what you can do," Cyclops said without taking his eyes away from the hole. "Hank, you keep Gambit supplied with ammunition."

From what Cyclops could tell through the swirling smoke, the Juggernaut was again on the very bottom of the hole. And from the looks of it, he was crouching.

Then suddenly the Juggernaut sprang upward, shoving as hard as he could with those huge legs.

Three quarters of the way up Cyclops hit the Juggernaut directly with a full blast, trying with everything he had to push him back down. Gambit smashed him with a large, kinetically charged brick.

The combined force of their attack stopped the Juggernaut's upward motion, but he shoved both feet and both hands deeply into the side of the pit, then started climbing.

Cyclops managed to vaporize the soil under his right side while Gambit sent explosion after explosion against the soil to his left.

And for a moment it looked as if it might work again. Cain started to topple over backwards.

But then, just at the last possible moment, the Juggernaut sank his legs firmly into the side of the pit, crouched, and sprang away from the wall, smashing into the other wall twenty feet under the two X-Men.

And in a position where they couldn't see the pit wall.

Before either of them could move around for an angle of attack, the Juggernaut was up and over the lip of the huge hole.

He turned and stared at Cyclops. "When I'm finished with this Service jerk, you're gonna pay for that little trick, Summers."

"Just trying to save your life, Cain," Cyclops said.

"You worry about your life," the Juggernaut said. "I'll take care of mine."

With that he turned and headed back for mansion.

At that moment Cyclops could see Service coming out of the side of the mansion, headed for the Juggernaut.

Only Phoenix stood between them now, and Cyclops doubted she had enough power to hold them apart very long.

Round two was about to begin and for some reason Cyclops didn't believe there would be a round three between the two giants.

Phoenix saw Service come through the mansion, then to her right she saw the Juggernaut emerge from the trap Cyclops and Gambit had built for him and head toward

Service. It looked as if it was now her turn.

In her mind she constructed the strongest telekinetic shield she could form and spread it between the two marching giants. She hoped it would be strong enough to keep the two titans apart.

Then a half-second before the Juggernaut hit it, Robert Service hit the shield and bounced back, surprised.

The Juggernaut did the same.

Storm and Bishop both hit Service, knocking him back away from the shield.

Cyclops and Gambit smashed at the Juggernaut, making him stagger back a few steps.

Again they both started forward, arms outstretched, ready to grab the other.

And again they hit the shield and bounced back.

Inside her mind, Phoenix could feel the enormous strain of holding the shield up against the two. She didn't know how many hits she could withstand.

Wolverine jumped onto the back of Service and started slashing with his claws.

Service grabbed Wolverine like he was nothing more than a dirty shirt and tossed him aside.

Rogue went in hard at the Juggernaut, but he smashed her away, sending her tumbling like a ball across the lawn and into a tree. Then, ignoring the constant barrage that Cyclops and Gambit flung at him, he moved up until he could feel the shield. Then with a mighty blow, smashed his fist into it.

Phoenix had seen the blow coming and braced herself, but it felt as if her mind was being ripped out through her eyes. Never in her life could she have imagined such pain.

Drop your shield, the Professor's voice echoed clearly in her head.

But—she started to object, but his voice filled every nook of her brain.

Now!

She did as he said just as the Juggernaut started to again swing at the shield.

There was nothing there for him to hit.

He moved forward and within moments he had a grip on the emerald on Service's chest.

And Robert Service, at the exact same time, had a grip on the ruby on the Juggernaut's chest.

Phoenix slumped to the lawn and sat watching. She had a terrible headache, but even through the pain she could hear the Professor's voice. *Jean, I have a plan that should allow us to finally end this.*

She nodded and hoped that the Professor's plan was a good one. They'd hit Service and Cain with everything they had, and it barely slowed them down.

Now it was do-or-die time.

CHAPTER 16

The Professor sat ridged in his hoverchair, his mind focused on what had just happened at the Service estate. Around him the even temperature of his study contrasted with the bizarre mix of heat, humidity, and cold that Storm's weather-working had brought to the Service estate.

He could also feel all the aches and torn muscles and bruises they were suffering at the moment. But thankfully, all of them were still alive and well.

He was also hurting from what he had felt just a moment before when Phoenix tried to hold Cain and Service apart.

But none of that mattered now. He'd finally located a text that gave him the final piece of the puzzle. He'd run a computer simulation, and now it confirmed his hypothesis. The answer had been staring them right in the face all along.

Now linked with the entire X-Men team on the Service estate, he could feel the minds of Wolverine, the Beast, Cyclops, Gambit, Rogue, Bishop, Storm, and Phoenix. They were all waiting, listening for him to begin.

"I have been able to find many references to the ruby of Cyttorak and the crimson bands of Cyttorak, but comparatively little on this emerald. However, I have found one text that talks of both the ruby and the emerald together, and it confirms what Gary Service told us.

"Both of them serve as conduits to Cyttorak, and are sources of great power. Originally they were placed in the two hands of a statue. A prophecy states that one day the statue would come alive and bring its hands together, which would bring about a new age, as the power of Cyttorak would flood into this world.

"However, while they are separated, only one can serve as a proper conduit for Cyttorak's power. Cain's power has gone unchallenged, since the emerald has been shattered for centuries. Now that the emerald is in use, it's taking power away from Cain, hence the pain he's been feeling."

Juggy don't seem like he's hampered none, Rogue said.

"I suspect that is due to Cain's lengthier relationship with the ruby. Service, for all his power, is still a neophyte. But the advantage may soon be his thanks, unfortunately, to us. You see, both jewels feed off of energy—that only increases their power."

So all our attacks have had the opposite effect of what we wanted, Cyclops said.

"Correct. The jewels work much the same way as Bishop's power."

Great, Wolverine said, *so how the hell do we stop 'em?*

"The same way the statue was destroyed. The emerald must be physically smashed."

Easier said than done, Charles, the Beast pointed out. *Our two overgrown playmates are going at it great guns once again. I doubt we could get through to the emerald to smash it.*

Yes we can, Cyclops said. *Professor, you said both jewels are energy conduits, yes?*

THE JEWELS OF CYTTORAK

"That is correct."

Then we can do it. Bishop, I want you to pull the same trick you pulled before. Absorb the energy field that Cain and Service are creating.

Bishop's thoughts felt dubious to the Professor. *I doubt they'll be distracted a second time.*

They won't need to be. You just need to absorb enough of the energy field to allow Phoenix to create a telekinetic wedge between them. It just needs to be enough to separate them for a moment.

The Professor saw where Cyclops was going with his plan. He didn't like it. "Cyclops, can I assume that you are proposing to fire on Cain's ruby?"

That's exactly what I'm proposing. Service has ripped open his armor, so the ruby is exposed. If Bishop, Storm, Gambit, and I hit the ruby with everything we've got, it should give Cain the upper hand and weaken Service enough to allow access to the emerald.

Yeah, but we already proved we can't blow it off him, Wolverine pointed out.

Blow it off, no. Smash it, yes. That's where you come in, Wolverine. Gary Service told us that the emerald, according to legend, was smashed by a wooden staff.

The Professor could feel Wolverine's smile through the link. *In that case, my claws should have no problem.*

The Professor hesitated. Cyclops's plan was sound, as always, but it meant increasing Cain's power.

But Robert Service was the greater threat here. Better the evil you know, as the saying went. If stopping Service meant increasing Cain's power, then that was what they had to do.

"Very well, X-Men. One thing, however. If you succeed in smashing the emerald back into its three parts, we must get those pieces away from there as quickly as possible, without touching them. And without letting Cain get them. They are too deadly."

You got dat right, Gambit said. *Dem t'ings messed up Remy's home.*

Understood, said Cyclops, and like thoughts came from the others.

"Good luck," he said.

Then he cut the link with the team. The strain was beginning to take its toll.

The dark coolness of his study closed in around him and he let himself sink down slightly in his hoverchair. He was worried, both for his team, and for the first time in years, for the life of his stepbrother.

If this didn't work, there would be no telling what Service might do to him. And that possibility the Professor didn't even want to think about.

And if it did work, the Juggernaut could become an even greater menace.

Whatever else had happened between them, Cain Marko was still family, and Charles Xavier could not bring himself to wish him ill. At least, not the level of ill that Robert Service would do to him if Cyclops's plan failed.

Cyclops took a deep breath of as the Professor cut the telepathic link. Then he glanced around at the fight going on between the Juggernaut and Robert Service. They were still just standing toe to toe, holding onto the other's gem, smashing at each other. Once again, a barrier of ionized air was forming around them.

Stalemate.

Well, he thought, *if this works, that'll be broken in a minute*.

Cyclops nodded to Bishop, who once again thrust his hands into the energy being generated by the two behemoths.

As Bishop had feared, it did not distract them this time. *Go, Jean*, Cyclops thought to his wife through the rapport they shared.

Scott Summers could see the frown of intense concentration on the face of the woman he loved as she tried to drive the combatants apart.

For a moment nothing happened. Service and Juggernaut continued to pound at each other, oblivious to Bishop's presence right next to them.

Then, just for a moment, they broke apart, looks of surprise on both their faces.

"Now!" Cyclops shouted.

Bishop, being the closest, was the first to fire, hitting the ruby with all the power he'd just accumulated.

Cyclops fired a beam as tight as the one he'd used to dig the trench earlier.

Storm sent a barrage of lightning.

Gambit had run out of cards, so he grabbed several rocks and branches and tossed them with unerring accuracy at Juggernaut's chest.

It looked for a moment like a miniature bomb had exploded in front of Cain Marko.

The Juggernaut screamed.

So did Robert Service.

Then, the X-Men's barrage still in full force, Juggernaut charged forward and bodyslammed Service, who landed fifteen feet away on his back.

"Cease fire!" Cyclops ordered, cutting off his optic blast. "Wolverine, now!"

To an observer unfamiliar with Wolverine, they would think that he was leaping onto the chest of a defenseless man and slicing his heart out.

But Cyclops knew Logan was more precise than that. With three precise swipes, he slashed at the emerald.

Service screamed once again, and slammed a fist into Wolverine's stomach that send the Canadian mutant flying back toward the estate. Rogue flew off to rescue him.

Then Service tried to get up.

There was a huge explosion of bright green light.

Force blasted outward, like a solid, invisible wall, smashing through the air and mowing down everything and everybody in its path.

Cyclops tumbled head over heels, coming up flat on the grass facing the lawn. The wind was knocked out of him, but he could still see what was happening to the two giants and his team.

Service tumbled three or four times, head over heels, then lay still on the grass. Right before Cyclops's eyes Service shrunk down to a normal size.

The Juggernaut was tossed a hundred feet backward,

landing with such force that he plowed a five-foot-deep trench in the lawn.

Rogue, while trying to retrieve Wolverine, was smashed into the house. Both of them ended up crashing through a second-story bedroom.

Storm managed to protect herself with her power and ride out the force wave.

Phoenix somehow had gotten a protective bubble around Gambit and herself, but no one else.

Hank was slowly picking himself out of a rose bush. Bishop had been thrown against a tree, but he too moved slowly.

And on the torn up-grass where the two combatants had just been fighting, three emeralds lay, shining in the afternoon sun.

Cain shook his head and managed to sit up.

He was a good distance from where he'd been fighting with Service. Most of the windows were blown out of the mansion and his stepbrother's annoying group were scattered around the huge lawn like child's toys tossed away. Granted, they had helped him feel stronger by feeding him energy. But that didn't make up for trapping him in that stupid hole.

He climbed to his feet and looked around.

Where was Service?

Then he noticed the naked, normal-sized man laying face down on the lawn and realized he had won.

He also realized the pain in his chest had stopped. It

had been there so long, it seemed, that he'd almost gotten used to it, like he'd almost gotten used to the beatings from his father.

But now, like his father, the pain was gone.

He could feel nothing. No drive to find anything. No direction to follow.

He was free again.

And he was going to make sure he stayed that way.

On the grass near where the naked man lay was the emerald, now in three pieces again. He would make sure that no one ever could hurt him again with that stone.

Ever.

Keeping his eyes focused on the stone, he started back toward where he and Service had fought.

Suddenly he was hit from the side by that annoying little furball, the Beast. He grabbed him and tossed him in the direction of the huge hole in the yard.

Then Storm faced him, holding up her hand for him to stop.

"No, Cain," she said. "Don't touch the stones."

He ignored her and kept going, now not more than twenty steps away from the largest of the emeralds.

Suddenly a huge wind was hitting him squarely in the chest, pushing him backward. He caught his footing and pushed forward, one step slow at a time.

Nothing was going to stop him.

Nothing.

Especially Charles's annoying little group.

• • •

"Storm!" Cyclops shouted with what breath he could muster, pushing himself back to his feet at the same time.

The Juggernaut was headed back for the emeralds. The Beast had tried to stop him and gotten brushed aside. Bishop stood before him, shortly joined by Rogue flying down with Wolverine from the second story, but he was still coming, getting closer and closer.

Someone had to move those emeralds. And the only one of them who could do that without touching them was Storm.

"Storm, blow the emeralds over by me, quickly!"

The Juggernaut had forced Rogue back almost to the emeralds now, and had smashed aside Bishop like he was nothing more than an annoying weed in his way.

Storm formed a wind with consummate ease—given the microblizzard and the tornado, the winds had already intensified to a degree most atypical for midsummer, so it was a simple matter for Ororo to give them a push.

Within seconds all three stones landed on the grass in front of him. That had bought them another twenty paces and a few more minutes.

Cyclops stared at the dangerous gems at his feet, then shouted to Phoenix who had joined the fight with Rogue to slow down the Juggernaut.

Suddenly, he heard the Professor's voice in his head. *Cyclops, quickly, you must blast the emeralds the same way you blasted the ruby.*

"But won't that increase their power?" Cyclops said.

And decrease Cain's. Do it!

Cyclops hesitated only for a second. Still, he had always trusted Charles Xavier in the past. He saw no reason to stop now.

Please, Scott—this may be our chance to finally end the menace of the Juggernaut.

Cyclops fired a wide optic blast at the three emerald fragments. At the same time, he directed an instruction at Phoenix to have Bishop, Storm, and Gambit once again join him, while the others were to keep the Juggernaut at bay.

They hit the fragments with everything they had.

"No!"

The shout came from the Juggernaut. Through his rapport with Phoenix, Cyclops could sense that Cain had brushed all four X-Men away with one tremendous blow and was now stomping toward the emerald.

The fragments started to glow an eerie green.

Juggernaut cried out again, this time in pain.

That's when Cyclops felt something gnawing at his mind . . .

Gary Service managed to crawl out of the remains of the side door of the mansion and stand. Outside, the Juggernaut and the costumed heroes stood around some kind of green glow. They looked like they were in a trance.

He looked around at the once-beautiful yard of the Service family estate. Now the place looked exactly like it was: a battlefield. It would take months, maybe years, and a lot of cash, to restore the grounds to their former glory.

Then Gary saw his brother, lying face down in the grass. At normal size.

His heart sank. *Did they kill him? Was there no other way?*

He ran over and knelt beside Robert. He wasn't breathing.

In college, Gary had taken a course in CPR. It had been years since he put those classes to use, but he wouldn't give up on Robert, not without a fight.

Slowly, Gary rolled his brother over onto his back. An ugly red burn covered the center of his chest, but otherwise he didn't seem to be injured.

He massaged the heart five times, right at the edge of the scarring from where the emerald had been. Then he grabbed Robert's nose, inhaled quickly, and breathed once.

He repeated the maneuver.

Five compressions. One breath.

Over and over again.

He lost track of how many times he did it.

Five compressions. One breath.

Then Robert coughed.

"Robert?" Gary said. "Robert, can you hear me?"

"What—what happened?" Robert said in a small voice. It was a complete contrast from the booming voice he had been using since first coming into contact with the emerald.

"How do you feel?"

"Awful. Did—did you save my life?"

Gary shrugged. "I guess I did, yeah."

"Why?"

"Because you're my brother."

Centuries ago, the power of Cyttorak seeped through the emerald situated in the right hand of a great statue and entranced two young monks with easily molded minds.

Then another monk shattered the emerald, and left its accompanying ruby buried.

But the power was still there.

And it was enticing.

It had enticed a lonely trapper in the Northwest Territories and given him eternal life.

It had enticed an ambitious construction worker in New Orleans and given him power to control the city.

And it had enticed a man who had spent his life being beaten down by his father and given him great strength.

Now the power of the emerald had lost its conduit. So it reached out once again. Just as the ruby that once rested in the statue's left hand had reached out to a weak young bully named Cain Marko and turned him into an unstoppable force, so did the emerald seek another like Albert Jonathan, Wingate Toole, and Robert Service.

Instead, it found the X-Men.

It found people who had faced the worst humanity had to offer. It found people who had overcome adversity, both physical and spiritual, and always come back.

It found people who knew the risks of absolute power, knew how it corrupted, and knew to resist it at all costs.

It found heroes.

THE JEWELS OF CYTTORAK

Phoenix, who carried the memories of a creature that took her form and personality and succumbed to near-absolute power to become a being of evil. Storm, who had once been worshipped as a goddess, and understood the pitfalls of trying to be a human deity. The Beast, the rationalist whose interest in the emerald was purely scientific, and who had seen too much as an X-Man, Avenger, and Defender to ever be tempted by the power of Cyttorak. Gambit, who had seen what the emerald had done to his hometown and rejected it outright. Wolverine, whose mind and body had been tampered with by forces outside his control and who would never willingly accept such again. Bishop, who came from a future where he lived under the yoke of absolute power. Rogue, who lived with the possibility, and the fear, of becoming something other than herself anytime she touched someone.

And Cyclops, the leader, who had fought for a dream of harmony among humans longer than any of them, for whom the idea of absolute power was anathema.

They all rejected the power.

But the power was still there. Building.

Building.

Until it exploded.

The last thing Rogue remembered was some kind of green explosion. Then there was something weird in her head, then *another* green explosion. Then nothing.

The next thing she knew, she woke up on the ruined grounds of the Service estate. The other X-Men were unconscious.

There was no sign of Robert Service.

However, Juggernaut was still present.

"How d'ya like that?" Cain said, staring at the ground.

Rogue followed his gaze to a huge hole of charred earth. She remembered that that's where the broken emerald was.

"Where'd it go?" she asked.

"Looks like it's gone. Even after it came offa Service's chest, I could feel it. But I don't feel nothin' now." He looked back at Rogue. "Far as I'm concerned, lady, this's over. I'm still pissed at you guys for puttin' me in that hole, but you guys destroyed the jewel, so I figure we're even, for now."

Rogue looked around. Wolverine was starting to stir, but none of the other X-Men were moving anytime soon. And she wasn't in any shape to take on the Juggernaut alone—or even with Wolverine, once he recovered.

"For now, yeah, we're even, Marko. 'Sides, we still owe ya for helpin' against Magneto, so we'll letcha go."

Juggernaut snorted. "You're all heart, girlie. Fact is, you couldn't stop me if you wanted. Just remember— nothin' stops the Juggernaut."

With that, Cain Marko simply walked off.

Gary hung up the phone and looked over at his brother, whom he'd placed on the couch, wrapped in a blanket. The ambulance would arrive shortly. What Gary had hoped would happen, had happened. Robert had returned to normal size and would spend time in jail for his crime, if he ever recovered from the shock.

And Gary would have control over the Service businesses. And the people who would benefit from that fact would be charity.

Lots and lots of charities.

EPILOGUE

The Professor floated through the cool rooms of the Institute on his hoverchair, moving silently into the study. The day had been a long one, but a successful one. Robert Service had been returned to normal, the emerald destroyed, and Cain calmed down. And no member of the team seriously hurt. Indeed, the team had overcome great temptation. He was proud of them.

In the study, Scott, Jean, Ororo, Remy, Rogue, and Bishop sat in chairs, sprawled out like the tired beings they were. Hank was already back hard at work in the lab and Wolverine had said he needed some time alone and had pulled one of his usual disappearing acts.

Scott and Jean sat side by side in the big overstuffed armchair. Rogue was in another of the big chairs and Remy rested on the arm of the chair beside her, his hand resting comfortably on her shoulder.

Storm had the couch to herself while Bishop sat straight in one of the smaller chairs, his eyes and mind clearly not focused on whatever banter the five others had been engaged in.

The Professor floated his chair up near the fireplace and faced his team. "Excellent work, everyone."

"We were lucky," Scott said. "If Cain had gotten that emerald, the world would be a different place."

"That it would," agreed the Professor. The thought of Cain having a hundred times the power he did now just made him shudder.

"Or if Service had beaten Cain," Jean said.

"Let's not even go into that possibility," Bishop said, his voice flat and clear.

"How's Robert Service doing?" Jean asked the Professor.

The Professor shook his head sadly. "Amazingly, he has already regained consciousness. But Gary Service told me just a few minutes before I came in here that Robert might be clinically insane."

"Insane?" Scott said. "You're kidding?"

"Enough of a shock will send anyone over the edge," the Professor said.

"Poor Gary," Rogue said. "Lost his father and now this with his brother, all in the same week."

The Professor suppressed a laugh. At the end of his phone call with Gary, he had offered to help fund the Institute. The Professor had turned him down politely, but the offer sounded as if Gary was doing just fine with his newfound wealth and power.

After a moment, Scott said, "I'm sorry we couldn't cure Cain. But the emerald fragments destroyed themselves before they had a chance to make any significant changes to him."

The Professor sighed. "Thank you, Scott, but it was a longshot. As I said, Cain and the ruby have been bonded to each other a long time now. It would take more than that to cure him of being the Juggernaut now." He hesitated. "But I had to make the attempt. After all, he is my brother."

"Family," Rogue said, shaking her head in disgust. "Too bad we can't pick our families, huh?"

The Professor glanced around the room at his team,

then smiled. "Sometimes, I think we can."

Scott and Jean both broke into broad smiles. They knew exactly what he meant. The X-Men were family. And one way or another, they all knew it.

He turned his hoverchair around and headed back for his study. Over his shoulder he said, "Dinner will be in one hour. Don't be late."

Then smiling to himself, he went back to work.

Two days later at Andreassi Memorial Hospital, Gary Service watched his brother through a one-way observation window. Beside him, Dr. Reeves stood, also watching.

Robert was strapped to his bed, a huge bandage on his chest where the emerald had been just a few days before. He was twisting back and forth, doing his best to break free. All the time swearing and holding a conversation with himself.

"I know it's early, Doctor," Gary said, staring at his brother, "but do you have any idea what's happened to him?"

The doctor nodded. "The preliminary diagnosis is that he's suffering from Multiple Personality Disorder."

Gary glanced at the doctor. "You're kidding? He's never shown any indications of that in the past."

"Perhaps, Mr. Service, but he's showing evidence of it now." He consulted Robert's chart. "In addition to his own personality, he's also modulated into two others. One is a fur trapper from Idaho, and the other is a—"

"A gangster from New Orleans," Gary said, finishing the doctor's sentence.

Reeves turned and faced Gary, his eyes cold and very serious. "I thought you said he had shown no indications of MPD in the past."

"He hasn't," Gary said, staring at his brother through the glass. "But a short while back Robert stole something very important from them both."

"Guilt, huh?" the doctor said softly. "That might help us treat him."

Gary took one more look at his brother, then turned to the doctor. "Do anything you can to help him. Money is no object. After all, he is the only family I have."

The doctor nodded. "I understand."

Gary only nodded at him, then headed out the door whistling softly to himself. His father's funeral was in two hours and there were still details that needed to be resolved. Details he'd always hoped to one day have to solve.

Family details.

Centuries ago, a monk shattered the emerald of Cyttorak. But it was not destroyed. Instead, it was scattered into the winds of time.

Two days ago, a mutant named Logan shattered the emerald of Cyttorak again. And again, it was scattered into the winds of time.

One fragment went two hundred years into the future. It appeared on the underside of a dead coral reef in the Atlantic Ocean near Key West.

The second fragment travelled twenty years, materializing in the foundation of a construction site in Kansas City, just as the concrete was being poured into it.

The third and final piece went a mere two weeks into the future in a trash bin resting behind an apartment building in Manhattan.

And the power waited once again.

DEAN WESLEY SMITH has sold around one hundred professional short stories and twenty novels, but he claims that, since he was a comic fan for years, his favorite of those were the ones, like this volume, based on comics. The others include two Spider-Man novels, *Carnage in New York* (co-authored with David Michelinie) and *Goblin's Revenge* (with a third on the way), the young-adult novel *Iron Man Super Thriller: Steel Terror*, and the novelization of the movie *Steel*. He has also published novels under his own name and under the name Sandy Schofield in the *Star Trek* and *Aliens* milieus, as well as in his very own universe. Besides Michelinie, he has collaborated with award-winning author Kristine Kathryn Rusch and *Star Trek: The Next Generation*'s Jonathan Frakes. He won the World Fantasy Award and has been nominated for the Hugo Award four times and the Nebula Award once.

Artamus Studios founding member and true believer **CHUCK WOJTKIEWICZ** proudly holds an M.M.M.S., F.O.O.M., and a valid artistic license. He lives and draws in North Carolina with his wife Marc, dog Megatron, and a growing squadron of balsa wood rubber-band-powered model airplanes.

CHRONOLOGY TO
THE MARVEL NOVELS AND ANTHOLOGIES

What follows is a guide to the order in which the Marvel novels and short stories published by Byron Preiss Multimedia Company and Boulevard Books take place in relation to each other. Please note that this is not a hard and fast chronology, but a guideline that is subject to change at authorial or editorial whim. This list covers all the novels and anthologies published from October 1994–June 1998.

The short stories are each given an abbreviation to indicate which anthology the story appeared in. **USM**=*The Ultimate Spider-Man*, **USS**=*The Ultimate Silver Surfer*, **USV**=*The Ultimate Super-Villains*, **UXM**=*The Ultimate X-Men*, and **UTS**=*Untold Tales of Spider-Man*.

If you have any questions or comments regarding this chronology, please write us.

Snail mail: Keith R.A. DeCandido, Marvel Novels Editor
Byron Preiss Multimedia Company, Inc.
24 West 25th Street
New York, New York 10010-2710.
E-mail: KRAD@IX.NETCOM.COM

—Keith R.A. DeCandido, Editor

"The Silver Surfer" [flashback] [USS]
by Tom DeFalco & Stan Lee
The Silver Surfer's origin. The early parts of this flashback start several decades, possibly several centuries, ago, and continue to a point just prior to "To See Heaven in a Wild Flower."

"Spider-Man" [USM]
by Stan Lee & Peter David
A retelling of Spider-Man's origin.

"Side by Side with the Astonishing Ant-Man!" [UTS]
by Will Murray

"The Ballad of Fancy Dan" [UTS]
by Ken Grobe & Steven A. Roman
"Do You Dream in Silver?" [USS]
by James Dawson
"Livewires" [UTS]
by Steve Lyons
"Arms and the Man" [UTS]
by Keith R.A. DeCandido
"Incident on a Skyscraper" [USS]
by Dave Smeds
    These all take place at various and sundry points in the careers of Spider-Man and the Silver Surfer, after their origins, but before Spider-Man married and the Silver Surfer ended his exile on Earth.

"Cool" [USM]
by Lawrence Watt-Evans
"Blindspot" [USM]
by Ann Nocenti
"Tinker, Tailor, Soldier, Courier" [USM]
by Robert L. Washington III
"Thunder on the Mountain" [USM]
by Richard Lee Byers
"The Stalking of John Doe" [UTS]
by Adam-Troy Castro
    These all take place just prior to Peter Parker's marriage to Mary Jane Watson.

"On the Beach" [USS]
by John J. Ordover
    This story takes place just prior to the Silver Surfer's release from imprisonment on Earth.

Daredevil: Predator's Smile
by Christopher Golden

"Disturb Not Her Dream" [USS]
by Steve Rasnic Tem
"My Enemy, My Savior" [UTS]
by Eric Fein

"Kraven the Hunter is Dead, Alas" [USM]
by Craig Shaw Gardner
"The Broken Land" [USS]
by Pierce Askegren
"Radically Both" [USM]
by Christopher Golden
"Godhood's End" [USS]
by Sharman DiVono
"Scoop!" [USM]
by David Michelinie
"Sambatyon" [USS]
by David M. Honigsberg
"Cold Blood" [USM]
by Greg Cox
"The Tarnished Soul" [USS]
by Katherine Lawrence
"The Silver Surfer" [framing sequence] [USS]
by Tom DeFalco & Stan Lee
    These all take place shortly after Peter Parker's marriage to Mary Jane Watson and shortly after the Silver Surfer attained his freedom from imprisonment on Earth.

Fantastic Four: To Free Atlantis
by Nancy A. Collins
"If Wishes Were Horses" [USV]
by Tony Isabella & Bob Ingersoll

"The Deviant Ones" [USV]
by Glenn Greenberg
"An Evening in the Bronx with Venom" [USM]
by John Gregory Betancourt & Keith R.A. DeCandido
    These two stories take place one after the other, and a few months prior to The Venom Factor.

The Incredible Hulk: What Savage Beast
by Peter David
    This novel takes place over a one-year period, starting here and ending just prior to Rampage.

"On the Air" [UXM]
by Glenn Hauman
"Connect the Dots" [USV]
by Adam-Troy Castro
"Summer Breeze" [UXM]
by Jenn Saint-John & Tammy Lynne Dunn
"Out of Place" [UXM]
by Dave Smeds
    These stories all take place prior to the Mutant Empire *trilogy.*

X-Men: Mutant Empire Book 1: **Siege**
by Christopher Golden
X-Men: Mutant Empire Book 2: **Sanctuary**
by Christopher Golden
X-Men: Mutant Empire Book 3: **Salvation**
by Christopher Golden
    These three novels take place within a three-day period.

"The Love of Death or the Death of Love" [USS]
by Craig Shaw Gardner
"Firetrap" [USV]
by Michael Jan Friedman
"What's Yer Poison?" [USS]
by Christopher Golden & José R. Nieto
"Sins of the Flesh" [USV]
by Steve Lyons
"Doom²" [USV]
by Joey Cavalieri
"Child's Play" [USV]
by Robert L. Washington III
"A Game of the Apocalypse" [USS]
by Dan Persons
"All Creatures Great and Skrull" [USV]
by Greg Cox
"Ripples" [USV]
by José R. Nieto
"Who Do You Want Me to Be?" [USV]
by Ann Nocenti

"One for the Road" [USV]
by James Dawson
These stories are more or less simultaneous, with "Child's Play" taking place shortly after "What's Yer Poison?" and "A Game of the Apocalypse" taking place shortly after "The Love of Death or the Death of Love."

"Five Minutes" [USM]
by Peter David
This takes place on Peter Parker and Mary Jane Watson-Parker's first anniversary.

Spider-Man: The Venom Factor
by Diane Duane
Spider-Man: The Lizard Sanction
by Diane Duane
Spider-Man: The Octopus Agenda
by Diane Duane
These three novels take place within a six-week period.

"The Night I Almost Saved Silver Sable" [USV]
by Tom DeFalco
"Traps" [USV]
by Ken Grobe
These stories take place one right after the other.

Iron Man: The Armor Trap
by Greg Cox
Iron Man: Operation A.I.M.
by Greg Cox
"Private Exhibition" [USV]
by Pierce Askegren
Fantastic Four: Redemption of the Silver Surfer
by Michael Jan Friedman
Spider-Man & The Incredible Hulk: Rampage (Doom's Day Book 1)
by Danny Fingeroth & Eric Fein
Spider-Man & Iron Man: Sabotage (Doom's Day Book 2)
by Pierce Askegren & Danny Fingeroth

Spider-Man & Fantastic Four: Wreckage (Doom's Day Book 3)
by Eric Fein & Pierce Askegren
The Incredible Hulk: Abominations
by Jason Henderson

Operation A.I.M. *takes place about two weeks after* The Armor Trap. *The "Doom's Day" trilogy takes place within a three-month period. The events of* Operation A.I.M., *"Private Exhibition,"* Redemption of the Silver Surfer, *and* Rampage *happen more or less simultaneously.* Wreckage *is only a few months after* The Octopus Agenda. Abominations *takes place shortly after the end of* Wreckage.

"It's a Wonderful Life" [UXM]
by eluki bes shahar
"Gift of the Silver Fox" [UXM]
by Ashley McConnell
"Stillborn in the Mist" [UXM]
by Dean Wesley Smith
"Order from Chaos" [UXM]
by Evan Skolnick
These stories take place simultaneously.

"X-Presso" [UXM]
by Ken Grobe
"Life is But a Dream" [UXM]
by Stan Timmons
"Four Angry Mutants" [UXM]
by Andy Lane & Rebecca Levene
"Hostages" [UXM]
by J. Steven York
These stories take place one right after the other.

Spider-Man: Carnage in New York
by David Michelinie & Dean Wesley Smith
Spider-Man: Goblin's Revenge
by Dean Wesley Smith
These novels take place one right after the other.

X-Men: Smoke and Mirrors
by eluki bes shahar
   This novel takes place three-and-a-half months after "It's a Wonderful Life."

Generation X
by Scott Lobdell & Elliot S! Maggin
X-Men: The Jewels of Cyttorak
by Dean Wesley Smith
X-Men: Empire's End
by Diane Duane
X-Men: Law of the Jungle
by Dave Smeds
X-Men: Prisoner X
by Ann Nocenti
   These novels take place one right after the other.

Spider-Man: Valley of the Lizard
by John Vornholt
Fantastic Four: Countdown to Chaos
by Pierce Askegren
   These novels are more or less simultaneous.

"Mayhem Party" [USV]
by Robert Sheckley
   This story takes place after Goblin's Revenge.

Spider-Man: Wanted Dead or Alive
by Craig Shaw Gardner

NOW AVAILABLE IN HARDCOVER
THE FIRST X-MEN HARDCOVER!
X-MEN
EMPIRE'S END
A NOVEL BY NEW YORK TIMES BEST-SELLING AUTHOR
DIANE DUANE
PUTNAM